Read the Warning Label First

B.M. Hardin

Savvily Published LLC

ISBN-10:0991528190

ISBN-13:978-0-9915281-9-6

Library of Congress Control Number

LCCN#2015904995

This book is solely a work of fiction. Any resemblance to any persons, places, events or locales are coincidental. The story is fictitious therefore a nothing more than a product of the author's imagination.

Acknowledgments

First, God has blessed me with this talent and it is to him that I give thanks and honor for allowing me to borrow such an extraordinary gift.

Secondly, I'd like to acknowledge my family. They have pushed me even when I didn't want to be pushed so to all of you I want to say thank you.

Lastly, I want to acknowledge all of those that help me with my writing. Whether it is editing, proofreading, reading and reviewing, all of you play a major role in my success and with helping me become a better writer and author. To you I say thank you.

B.M. Hardin-

Twitter @BMHardin1

Facebook: www.facebook.com/authorbm

Email: info@savvilypublished.com Attention: BM Hardin

Read the Warning Label First-2015

Dedication

This book is dedicated to my sisters: Shanta McDowell, Cassandra Jackson, Tangela Brown, Angela Houser and Bethany Campbell (best friend). Though life takes us all on our own journeys, trials and though there are many roads that we all have to travel alone, I am and will always be my sister's keeper.

Love you guys to the moon and back and this one is dedicated to all of you!

~Smooches~

Read the Warning Label First

Chapter One

Love and happiness...

Makes me sick!

Don't you just hate when you see the perfect little couple, all in public, acting all perfect and stuff?

I mean just all over each other, kissing, touching and hugging in front of *us* single folks like its okay.

It's disrespectful if you ask me.

Get a room or something already...geesh!

Okay, so maybe I do have a little bit of misplaced anger when it came to love and there was no denying that I was just a tad bit jealous and periodically lonely.

But all of that is beside the point.

People should be more considerate of single people, instead of reminding people like me, of what we didn't have.

I hope they break-up---like today, I thought, as I hurriedly walked around the couple that was holding hands and giggling as though nothing else in the world mattered.

Obviously to them, nothing and no one else did.

What I wouldn't give to live that fantasy...but then again, my reality wasn't all that bad either.

I was one sexy, intelligent, successful black woman, with no kids, my own house and a career that most people only dreamed about.

So, yes, my reality was actually quite splendid; except maybe the lack of a love life.

Did I have a man?

Nope, I sure didn't.

But it wasn't because I couldn't get one.

Trust me, I could definitely get one.

I guess the truth was that I kind of, on *most* days, didn't want one.

I know, I know, many women say that if they wanted a man they could have one, but unlike most of them I was actually telling the truth!

Let me explain something, you see without a man, I could spend all of my money, when, where and how I wanted to. No questions asked, no splitting anything down the middle, it was my funds to do as I pleased.

On top of that, I could do what I wanted to do without having to check in with anyone or having to ask permission. My time was *my* time and I didn't have to be considerate with how or where I spent it.

Oh, but most importantly, I preferred to be single because being by myself meant that I didn't have to deal with all of the *extra* that came along with being in a relationship these days.

You know what I mean by *extra* right?

The lying, the cheating, the side chicks and let's not forget the baby mama drama.

Mentally, I just wasn't built for the nonsense. I'll be the first to admit that a few of my screws were just a tad bit loose and there was no telling what kind of trouble I would be in if I had to deal with some of the mess that other women put up with these days just to hear the words I love you.

No, thank you, I'll pass.

I tell myself "I love you" everyday anyway, so I hear it just as much as anybody else.

Self –love is the best love; you better ask somebody!

No one will ever love you better or more than you can love yourself. And believe it or not, people can tell.

No, but seriously, if being single meant being sane, then I would be cuddling with my satin sheets and my over-sized pillows for the rest of my life.

Or get a dog or a cat or something.

I'd worked too hard to be where I was in life and I wasn't going to get side tracked by chasing that little thing that we called love.

In a way, to me, it just wasn't worth it.

Nothing was worth my peace of mind. It was hard enough keeping it when it came to my line of work.

I worked in Accounting.

Short description, I was very, very good with numbers and twice as good at making companies and other people money.

I made six figures a year, and I knew without a shout of a doubt that I'd earned and that I deserved every single penny of it.

I was proud to say that I was the Senior Vice President at the best darn accounting firm in all of Washington, D.C.

I'd started at the bottom, and I'd worked my way to the top with patience, hard work and determination. There were only three people in positions that were higher than mine, and if you asked me, I was probably better at the job then all of them were.

I was damn good if I must say so myself. And I didn't mind tooting my own horn.

Toot. Toot.

Seriously though, I loved everything about my job.

Most thought being a top executive meant that I didn't have to do any hard work but that was a lie. I worked my ass off, more so than most of the people at the company.

Besides, some of the clients would only work with me. They trusted me and trusted my opinion.

But all and all, I loved the people, my position, my clients and especially my corner office.

I was born to do what I did and I gave it my all every single day.

I'd worked hard for everything that I had and I was finally reaping the benefits of my labor.

I liked expensive things and I bought whatever made me happy, or at least whatever would make me feel good at that moment.

Trust me, I had no problem admitting that work, stability, and a big bank account were my top priorities; but it was by choice, at least for now anyway.

Since I was getting older, I was sure that my priorities in some folk's eyes were all mixed up, but the order of importance of things was currently working just fine for me.

And as far as I was concerned, life was good.

And though most people didn't believe me, for the most part, I was just fine.

Finally outside, I hastily got into my car and I drove away as if I had something important to do.

I didn't.

No plans, no man...just me.

I'd only gone out because I was once told that in order to be seen, you had to be on the scene. Even if you weren't exactly looking, someone could very well be looking for you.

So, I always forced myself to get out and try new things and go to different places, in hopes of meeting new people.

In only an hour tops, I'd been approached three times, by men that shouldn't have dared to even come my way.

I hadn't given them more than a second or two of my time before I'd made it clear that I wasn't interested.

Men were a lot bolder than they used to be, but I was the wrong one to take a chance on if you didn't have your stuff together.

If you didn't step correct, you were simply going to end up with your feeling hurt.

Rejection is a bitch ain't it?

Arriving home, I thought about what it would be like to come home to a husband and a house full of kids. I guess it would have been nice, at times, to be greeted with smiles, hugs and kisses from those who were supposed to love you the most, especially on a night like tonight.

I couldn't lie, the thought was nice.

But in order for that to happen, the whole husband and kids' thing, not only would I have to *find* a decent man, which was a hell of a task all by itself, but I would also have to finally allow someone to meet the little *lady in pink* that lived in between my thighs.

That's right, I was knocking on the door of thirty and I wasn't ashamed to say that I was still a virgin.

My *good stuff* had never even been touched by anyone other than myself.

A piece of *wood* had never even come close to swimming in my *pool of ecstasy*.

No, I wasn't embarrassed by it and I didn't mind letting it be known that I was a virgin either.

I'd been raised by Christian parents.

And believe me, when I say that they were Christians, I mean C-H-R-I-S-T-I-A-N-S.

I'm telling you, they were the real deal.

They were so saved that you would have thought that they personally sat with Jesus himself, at the Last Supper, and broke bread.

The lived and breathed every word in the Good Book.

My parents were so saved that every question and every answer involved Jesus and his *peoples*.

Don't believe me?

Do you think that I am exaggerating?

Unfortunately I'm not.

For example, I could ask a simple question:

"Mama, how is the weather? Is it hot or cold outside today?"

And her response would have been:

"Well, it's a beautiful day that the Lord has made. Rejoice and be glad in it."

What?

That is not what I asked you! I asked you about the weather ma'am!

But that's just how it was and that's not even the half of it!

My parents followed every word in the Bible and coming up as a child they'd pushed so much religion into me that I was terrified to do anything that I even thought might be a sin.

It was clear that in their house, we followed their rules. And it wasn't up for debate or discussion.

We attended church at minimum, five days a week, and that's not to mention the in-home Bible studies and other things of that nature.

But once I went off to college and found out that I wasn't going to drop dead and go straight to Hell if I did something wrong or if I committed a sin here or there, I decided to let my hair down and live a little.

I found out that there were so many things that I didn't know. There were so many things that I hadn't seen and that I hadn't been exposed to.

Not saying that being sheltered is all bad, but because of my upbringing, I learned quickly once in college that I didn't know a damn thing, about anything!

So, naturally, I tried a few new things. I really got to know who I was as an individual, instead of being who my parents' trained me and told me to be.

But still yet, some things about me stayed the same.

Some of my standards and morals remained as they were and one thing that never changed was that I refused to give any man my most *prized possession* until they were deemed a worthy recipient of it.

I wasn't exactly sure if I was waiting for marriage or if I was just waiting for something that I could define as or that at least felt *real*.

Married or not, only true love would make me spread these legs!

Though holding out for marriage wouldn't be a bad thing, the jury was still out on that decision but I didn't have to decide right now.

But so far, every man that I'd ever dated had failed the test. They hadn't been worthy of all of me.

I had yet to find a man special enough or even deserving enough of my heart, my commitment, or my panties.

And at this point in my life I didn't have time, patience or even the energy to even think about giving it to anyone other than my Mr. Right.

So, as for now, I was simply untouched and *impatiently* waiting.

Virgin and all, I'd say that I'd had a pretty active dating life and I'd dated all types of men.

I'd dated white men, black men, Latino men and hell, even an Irish man once.

Christian men, professional men, educated men and I'd even tried the successful, dread wearing, vegetarian, in tune with the sun and the moon type of guy, but I had yet to find the *one*.

When those men didn't seem to work out, I'd even tried bending on my necessities, just a little, to the middle class working, mill laborer, car servicing, or fork-lift driving type of guy.

But still, I had no luck with finding someone that I thought was good enough to keep around forever.

Nothing was ever just right.

Everybody said that I was too picky and that I was going to be alone forever, but to be honest, I'd take being alone, with dignity, over being used, hurt, disrespected or having to share a baby's daddy with two or more women, on any given day.

Oh hell no, again...Tori will pass on that one.

I definitely wasn't sharing my *special pussy-pop* just to end up in Hell on earth.

I just couldn't do it.

Call me naïve, stuck-up, full of it, or whatever you want to, but the right man for me was out there, somewhere, and hopefully he would come my way soon.

If what my mother had preached all of that time was true, the man that was supposed to have me, was waiting for me, searching for me, and when he found me, I was going to be ready.

But for the time being, I had to settle for a good ole' *Bo.*

When I tell you that every woman needs a *Bo*...that's exactly what I mean!

Bo was my *toy* and *main-thang* at the moment.

Say what you want but *Bo* and a drawer full of batteries were the best thing to ever happen to me and it was getting the job done just fine.

Humph, don't judge me!

And surely don't knock it until to you try it.

I'd been like that at one point in my life, but it had surely made a fool out of me.

Some would ask me how did I know what I was missing if I'd never had it?

The truth was, I didn't know.

I couldn't exactly say what it was that I was missing, but I was still a woman and I got urges just like everyone else.

For years I'd dealt with this *itch* that I just couldn't scratch and since I wasn't too fond of trying to figure it out with my fingers the old fashioned way, I turned to modern day technology instead.

Not to mention that I wasn't too fond of the whole idea of masturbating, or self-pleasing but something had to be done before I went insane.

So, One day, after a long night of feeling what I presume to be horny, the next morning, in a hoodie sweatshirt and with sunglasses on, I went to the adult store and I got myself a *Bo*.

And *we* have been in a committed *relationship* ever since.

Hell if I could marry *him*, I probably would!

And I was so not joking either.

Okay, so maybe I enjoyed it a little too much and maybe I was even a little addicted to it, but for now, it was just going to have to do.

It was my only option.

But one thing was for sure, if the *real thing* was anything like *Bo,* then I knew that once I got just a taste of it, I was going to be in big trouble.

Entering the house, immediately, I took off my clothes and made myself comfortable on the couch.

There was truly no place like home.

After relaxing for just a second or two, I grabbed my laptop and I checked a few emails.

Everything from work I ignored.

I hate mass e-mails.

Work was the last thing on my mind, especially since I didn't have to go back for a while.

I checked a few other miscellaneous things and even decided to *semi-internet stalk* a few of my ex's on social media.

I never bothered them or anything.

I just looked to see what they were up to in their lives. Basically, I was looking to see if they had found love.

Some of them had.

Some of them were now married with children and I couldn't help but wondered if they had become better men since they'd dated me.

For the wives sake, I sure hope so.

After I was done being nosey, I picked up my phone and scrolled through my contacts to see who I could call.

Once I reached the end of my contacts list, I got an idea. I was finally going to give a guy from work a call.

His name was Vick.

He was new to the company and since I was the *best*, I'd had the pleasure, well more like the responsibility of showing him the ropes.

Of course he didn't make more money than I did, but he made enough to put him in the category of being a *potential*.

Anyway, he'd approached me on several occasions with his lines and compliments and I'd finally decided to take his number a few days ago.

I'd yet to call him and since I had been on vacation from work for the past two days and I would be for the next two weeks, I hadn't had to see him to give him an excuse or explanation.

But today was as good as ever.

I was bored to death and I wasn't doing anything, so I took a deep breath and tapped my finger on his number to call him.

"Hey Vick, it's me, Tori."

"Who? Oh, hey *you*---um, can I call you back? I'm kind of busy," Vick said and he'd barely let me respond before he hung up.

How rude!

I looked at the phone as I removed it from my ear.

And there it goes...

There goes the sign.

There's goes the big red flag.

And one red flag was all that I needed.

See, some women fail to see the signs when they are clearly already there.

They try to write them off as coincidences or *maybe* he's telling the truth, but not me.

I always paid attention, to everything, and if there was something there for me to see, you had better believe that I was going to see it.

I always *read the warning labels, first,* before getting into something that my heart might not be able to get me out of.

To date, though I'd dated many men, I'd never truly been in love.

I'd been in strong *like* a time or two, but never had I been deeply and fully in love.

There was just always something that I would see ahead of time, before going *there*...and I would always be right.

So, I'd do us both a favor and save myself the headache, heartache and maybe even a trip to jail or to the clinic, if it would have even gotten that far, by removing myself from the equation.

To me, it was just that simple.

So as for Vick, just like that, my mind was now programmed to say...*Vick* who?

And once my mind was made up about a man, there wasn't a thing that he could do to change it.

Hell, he even called me *you* instead of saying my name.

Dead giveaway that he was in the presence of someone that he couldn't address me properly in front of.

Did he think that I was stupid?

He would have come out better by just not answering my phone call. At least it would have still given him a little lead way for some type of chance.

I headed to delete Vick's number, but decided that I should let him spend the two weeks that I was out off of work on the block list.

That way I didn't make the mistake of answering his number.

There was nothing that I needed to say to him, over the phone that is, and there was surely nothing else that he had to say to me.

But best believe as soon as I saw him, I was going to tell him not to waste anymore of my time and to stay the hell out of my space and definitely out of my face.

Honestly, I wasn't disappointed.

If anything, I was thankful that the sign had shown up when it had and that I hadn't had to waste much of my time.

Like I said, the man for me was still out there.

I guess Vick just wasn't him.

Thinking only a second longer, finally, I shrugged my shoulders, threw my phone down on the couch and headed to my bedroom to relieve some of my *frustrations.*

Why couldn't every man be like my *Bo?*

***

"What about him?"

"Nope, he's faking. He's a liar---and he's broke."

"How can you tell all of that just by looking at him?"

"His suit is a knock off, and he's wearing a watch that's shining so bright from the fake diamonds that they seemed to be striving to take over the Sun's position. He's lying about who he is to fit in with the men that he thinks those men are; which makes him a liar. Oh, and did I mention that he's broke," I concluded with a smirk, paid for my vanilla expresso and walked out of the shop with Delilah hot on my trail.

"You don't know that."

"Know what? Oh, the suit was definitely a knock off and I've seen enough real watches to know what a fake one looks like," I giggled.

Whether she wanted to admit it or not, she knew that more than likely...I was right.

"Well, everyone can't be at the same pay rate as you, you know," my assistant Delilah responded as though her comment had come from a personal place in her heart.

"I don't expect them to be. But I was taught that men are the providers, and that's what I expect them to do. Even if I do make more than him, I have to know that if times get tough he can play his role and provide for us all on his own. Is that too much to ask?" I said as we walked into the work building.

"In this day in time? Maybe."

We chatted for a few minutes more and then went our separate ways.

No sooner than I'd turned the corner there he was. Vick.

"I've been calling you back to back, since that night that you called, but you never picked up," he proclaimed.

I just stared at him silently.

"So, what happened? Did you get busy or something? How was your vacation?"

I took a deep breath.

"Vick, look, don't call me again. Better yet don't even speak to me unless it is work related. Thanks," I waved at him as I turned and walked away.

Once inside of my office, immediately, I found my phone and deleted his number.

No need for blocking him anymore.

I'm sure that I'd made myself crystal clear.

I hadn't given him a chance to say anything because there was nothing from him that I needed to hear.

He could just move on to the next woman.

Maybe she wouldn't mind being his side *piece.*

Sitting the phone down on my desk, I frowned at the amount of paper work stacked in neat, medium sized piles in front of me.

Two and a half weeks of vacation hadn't been long enough. The days had been spent doing much of nothing but I felt as though I needed just a few more days.

I loved my job I really did, but taking my first vacation in what seemed like forever, reminded me that even I needed a break sometimes.

And I would definitely be taking a break here or there a lot more often.

With a full day ahead of me, I took off my blazer and took a sip of my Heaven in a cup.

Okay, let's do this...

The day went by painfully slow and I couldn't wait until the clock struck five o'clock.

I usually stayed late, but that just wasn't going to happen today.

I'd taken care of every item that was on my desk and this chick here was exhausted!

Grabbing my things, I ran out of the office...literally.

Vick saw me heading out the door and looked like he wanted to head in my direction, but if he knew what was best for him he would just keep it moving.

I didn't need any excuses or explanations.

Trust me, none were needed and there wasn't a thing that he could say that would make me give him another chance.

Nine times out of ten, he was already involved with someone else and that was his business---and absolutely none of mine.

But instead of being up front about it, he was just like *some* men.

He'd rather have his cake and eat it to.

But I was the wrong woman to try and run game on.

I was one of the few women who knew her worth and I wasn't afraid to be alone until someone was willing to give me the love that I deserved.

Nice try though.

Safely in my car, I was driving in silence, and thinking about love.

I suddenly thought about going to see my mother.

My mother, Sadie, was, well...she was something I tell you.

She was a woman of so many strengths but she only had one weakness.

My father.

As surprising as it may sound, especially because of their beliefs, my parents actually divorced my last year of high school.

To be honest, I think that the divorce was actually the start of my rebellion.

I'd always been taught that marriage was supposed to be until death, and that divorce was frowned upon, but then one day, my mother did the unthinkable.

She sat everything that my father owned on the other side of our front door.

The funny thing was...he didn't give a damn.

He hadn't even had the nerve to come and get his things, instead he sent my uncle.

To think about it, he'd never made the attempt to come to the house, he'd talked to my mother about the situation over the phone.

But mama didn't want to hear anything that he had to say.

She divorced his ass.

Though it wasn't exactly what I'd been preached all of my life, I couldn't blame her.

My father had been messing around on her with a lady from the church for years.

Of course I saw the signs, but my mother refused to believe that my father was capable of something like that until the woman's husband, Deacon Davis, knocked on our front door.

He'd said the most interesting thing that day.

The Deacon found it strange that his wife was now twelve weeks pregnant again, but the problem was that due to dealing with a few issues regarding Crons Disease, he'd said that he hadn't even touched her in over six months.

Unable to deny the obvious, she confessed to the affair with my father and the Deacon had come to inform my mother.

I remembered it as if it had only happened yesterday.

The look on my mother's face was so full of disappointment. The pain in her eyes that day was a vision that I would remember for a lifetime.

She was so, so sad, while on the other hand I couldn't believe that she'd missed it.

My father rarely touched her or even looked at her. I strongly believed that he was trying his best to stay around because of his beliefs and because of us, their five kids, but I guess his flesh won a few battles that his mind and heart had always told him that he could conquer.

With no hesitation, my mother divorced him and he moved on quickly with a new wife and a new baby. Today, my father, stepmother slash the Deacon's ex-wife, and my twelve year old brother, lived far away somewhere out in Texas.

We never saw him, and rarely heard from him since he'd moved away.

It used to bother us all quite a bit; he was our father and had always been around. But somewhere, after some time, we all simply stopped caring.

I know for me, I most times just pretended that he was dead. It made it easier for me to cope with.

My mother, on the other hand, after the divorce, turned her focus back to religion and nearly drove herself insane.

Literally.

Over the years, the combination of heartache and religion had drove her mind to some place far away, and no matter what we tried, we couldn't get her to come back to us.

So, on the income of three of her five children, she was now in a very expensive *hospital* as they called it, where they were trying to help her get back on track.

But for the amount of bucks that it was costing us, it just didn't seem to be working.

Though I faithfully paid my share and though I wasn't my mothers' biggest fan, I'd always wanted her to live with me.

I wanted to take care of her.

In a way, I thought that it would be beneficial to the both of us but the doctors insisted that the hospital was in her best interest.

I hated to see her like that and here lately it was as though the medicines had her so spaced out that she hardly recognized any of us these days.

I had two older sisters, one older and one younger brother as well; not including the brother that my father and his mistress produced.

All of my siblings were married, with kids, and either doing average or pretty damn good for themselves.

I was the only one still searching for that someone special and hopefully that special guy was still searching for me.

Concluding my thoughts about my family, I decided that calling my mother instead of going by to see her was just as valid, since she probably wouldn't even know who I was.

Making a mental note to call her once I was home and settled, I headed to the grocery store instead.

Since I lived alone and rarely had company, I ate out most of the time but I could cook like nobody's business. I could whip up a nice, home-cooked meal with little to nothing; quick, fast and in a hurry.

But I rarely got the opportunity to show off my skills.

That is one thing, other than Jesus, that my mother had managed to teach me.

I could remember being able to fry a piece of chicken to perfection at only eight years old. I could bake almost anything from scratch by the time that I was ten.

Here lately, I had been craving meatloaf, so I figured that it was about time that I made me one, even though half of it would probably go to waste.

As soon as I started to push the cart, I realized that maybe I should have gone home to change first, or at least changed my shoes.

The four inch suede pumps weren't exactly fit for the task of grocery shopping, but I was going to tough it out and get it over with as fast as I could.

"Let me guess, you don't own a pair of sneakers?" he said.

Actually, he was right, I didn't, but instead of answering him, I turned to face him and grinned.

"Mike."

"Tori."

"Single?"

"Guess."

"Smart ass?"

"Mostly."

He couldn't help but to laugh.

Quickly I *appraised* him from top to bottom.

He was casually dressed, neatly groomed, and he smelled good too.

He surely wasn't the finest man that I'd ever seen, but his smile was hypnotizing and so for the time being, he had my attention.

For the next few minutes, Mike, followed me around the grocery store, like a dog in heat.

I listened to the way that he talked and to his vocabulary and I concluded that he had to be well educated; either that or he had been raised by parents that were.

His sense of humor was refreshing and I enjoyed the fact that he looked at my eyes more than he looked at my breasts.

Hmm...we might be on to something.

Once we were both finished shopping, he carried my bags and his outside.

Nice gesture, though if he'd really wanted to impress me, he would have paid for them too.

But I wasn't complaining.

He loaded my bags into the car and I smiled at him.

"So, I take Visa or MasterCard for my services. I only take debit. Don't write me a check because it might bounce," he smiled.

Never.

Never would my check bounce.

I couldn't help but smile at him.

He was definitely funny.

"Well, if you don't want to pay me, I guess your number will do. I mean since you put me to work and all, it's only fair that I get something out of the deal right?" he asked.

Boy did I love a man that could keep a smile on my face.

I continued to beam as I reached out my hand for him to place his cell phone in it but...

"Oh, I don't have phone right now. I have to pay the bill when I get paid on next week. I can call you off my *folk's* house phone though. Can you write it down on a piece of paper for me?" he said.

I forced myself to keep smiling and I tried my best to hide my disappointment, but I was only able to keep it together for all of three seconds.

If he couldn't pay a cell phone bill, on time, what on earth was he going to do with a woman like me?

Maybe it was a little shallow, but I didn't want to waste his time and I definitely didn't want him wasting mine.

What I needed was a *real* man.

And anything less than just wouldn't do.

Instead of reaching for a pen and paper, just as he started to talk again, I rolled up my car window and without looking in his direction, I proceeded to drive off.

I rolled my eyes at the sight of him in my rearview mirror, standing with his hands up in the air.

The nerve of him!

He was old enough to know that you don't approach a woman like me if you don't have all of your ducks in a row.

I exhaled loudly and turned up my radio.

Thank you God for the signs...

****

Chapter Two

"Did anyone ever tell you that you work too much?" Hunter, my boss, asked.

Hunter was a sexy, arrogant white guy, in his late forties.

He made twice my salary, yet he didn't have half of my intelligence or do half of the work that I did.

I was ten times better at the job than he was but he had been there twice as long as I had.

Hunter was married with kids---and he had a mistress.

The funny thing was, his wife walked around smiling as if she'd won the lottery or something but the reality was...she was just plain stupid.

She believed everything that he told her when all she really had to do was open her pretty blue eyes and see him for the scumbag that he really was.

Why was everyone so afraid of the truth?

The truth, to me, was better than a lie on any given day.

Why live your life full of lies when you could live a life of truth and honesty?

I just didn't see the joy in that.

From the very beginning, years ago at my interview, I knew that he was scandalous.

The way that he talked and chuckled after he thought that he'd said something funny or flattering. From the way that he licked his lips, slyly grinned and looked at me out of the corners of his eyes when he thought that I wasn't paying any attention.

Not only did he have all of the signs of a cheater but also those of a stalker or maybe even a serial killer.

But hey, what do I know?

But I wasn't sure if his wife even cared that he *serviced* other women in his spare time.

She seemed to be all about the money anyway.

It's amazing how people will choose stability and comfort over love and respect.

I will never understand.

There wasn't enough money in the world for me to allow a man to cheat on me, *knowingly*, and use me at his disposal.

I just couldn't do it.

After small talk and once his late in the evening phone call came through as always, my boss excused himself from my office, and I was left there alone.

I worked until my eyes told me that if I didn't leave at that very moment, I would be spending the night in my office again.

Walking out of my office, I heard the sound of an angel.

The night janitor was busy at work and singing like nobody's business.

The tone of his voice was so rich that it almost sent me into a trance. He could sing the average woman right out of her panties.

Luckily, I wasn't average.

"I could listen to you sing all night," I said aloud.

"Really? I would consider it an honor to sing to you all night Miss. Young," he answered me but didn't bother to look in my direction.

I smiled at him even though he wasn't looking at me. Though I didn't know his name, I'd seen him on most nights that I worked late, here recently.

He was fairly new, I think.

He seemed like a nice guy. I always made sure to speak to him because I felt that with him being surrounded by people with so much money, he had to feel some type of way about having to pick up their trash and clean up after them on a daily basis.

The least that we could do was speak to him and say thank you.

He wasn't dateable, but I wanted him to know that he was appreciated.

He was rather young to be a janitor, but I never bothered to ask him any personal questions.

As I exited the building, he stopped doing what he was doing to look out the window as always, to make sure that I made it safely to my car.

Once I was safely inside, he turned his back to the glass and continued mopping the floor.

Sweet...

If only he wasn't a janitor.

No, I wasn't a gold digger, but I was realistic.

The man that would be lucky enough to call me *his* would bring just as much to the table as I did.

And I couldn't, or maybe it was that I wouldn't apologize for having some kind of requirements and standards.

I'm telling you, I would live the rest of my life alone before I changed some of them.

And I meant that with everything in me.

***

"Don't you look good enough to eat? That dress is going to catch you somebody's man tonight. It damn sure better not catch you mine!" Donna laughed.

Donna was a friend of my assistant, Delilah, and I had become quite fond of her.

She was witty, funny and brutally honest.

And I mean as honest as they came; but I liked it.

I'd met Donna through Delilah over a year ago.

Let me say this, Delilah was my *friend* first, who needed employment, so I gave her the job as my assistant once I got my promotion.

It was no secret that Delilah didn't like the position, hell I wasn't even sure if she really even liked me.

Really, I should know better than to refer to her as a friend. Maybe associate was a better term for her.

Sometimes she was the one person that I could say that was always there for me, but I was no fool. I knew that she was jealous of me, and always had been though she didn't really have a reason to be.

Sure, I made way more money than she did, but I never threw my money or my bank account in her face. If anything, I was always trying to help her and push her to follow her dreams so that she didn't have to spend the next five years of her life working for me.

Delilah and I had been introduced a few years ago. We briefly dated friends.

But clearly they weren't worth keeping otherwise they would still be around.

Anyway, she and I became friendly.

It had only taken me about two see a few signs and the friend that I was dating, was history. But Delilah and I remained acquainted and shortly after meeting, Delilah popped up pregnant.

The said thing was that the friend that she had been dating turned out to be a deadbeat and neglected to take care of his responsibilities.

Even I missed that about him.

In the little time that I'd been around him, he hadn't come off as a man that wouldn't take care of his kids.

But the proof was in the pudding.

Just like that, Delilah was a single mother with a now a three year old son and currently looking for a man to play the role as a father figure in his life.

She'd made me his god mother but I was sure that it was only because she knew that I could back her financially when it came to him, which I did with no questions asked.

I loved him as if he was my own son, but I always slept with one eye open when it came to his mama.

It was just the vibe that Delilah gave off; not all the time, but enough for me to notice.

Maybe it wasn't as serious as I thought it was, but like I said, I paid attention to signs not only in men but in women as well and she gave all the signs that said: *Warning: Proceed with caution with this bitch.*

I'm just saying.

But now Donna, her best friend, and now a good friend of mine, was the truth and I liked the sincerity of her personality.

Donna was in a relationship, not a committed one, but one that she'd stated on several occasions that it worked for her.

She was with a cheater, but she knew it and she didn't care because she did whatever it was that she wanted to do too.

Basically, they had two kids together, and neither of them seemed to like the idea of another woman or another man being around them so, they just entertained others on the side.

I guess that was the most accurate way of putting it.

Hey, if they liked it, I loved it, but that kind of relationship just wasn't for me.

Hell to be real about it, it shouldn't have been for them either. Clearly they'd forgotten that STD's are real. That's all I'm saying.

But nevertheless, we were preparing to hit the town as two and *a half,* single ladies and hoping to have a little fun and maybe even meet someone new.

I was the thinner one of the bunch.

I didn't have much of anything, but I guess I had enough.

My breasts were bigger than my booty; which I had been meaning to get that fixed.

I had the funds for any type of surgery that I wanted. I was just a firm believer of the saying that if it wasn't broke, don't fix it.

And it would be just my luck that I bought a new booty and ended up with some rare and crazy side effect.

That was the only reason I hadn't gotten me a new, and bigger ass as of yet.

But it was still on my to-do list.

Other than the lack of booty, everything else was pretty much a go.

I was average height, brown skinned complexion and average length hair.

I was one of those people that didn't have all of the assets but I damn sure knew how to be sexy.

I had sex appeal which continuously made it easy for me to be noticed; if only I could be noticed by the right one.

But needless to say, getting approached had never been a problem, even when I was the odd ball out.

Donna and Delilah were both very shapely.

They were pretty much the same size from the top all the way down to their big round bottoms.

Delilah was definitely the prettier of the two, but her personality sucked which made Donna more desirable and attractive over her on any given day.

But nevertheless, we set out to laugh and drink the night away.

I could already tell that the night was going to go *sideways* just from the constant phone calls between Donna and her mate.

She was constantly explaining her destination and reminding him that she allowed him to have his free time so that he needed to back off so that she could enjoy herself. But for some reason, on this particular night, he seemed to be all in his feelings.

Maybe he was tired of the games that they were playing...

Yeah right!

Donna said that he was only being clingy because his side chick had dumped him.

I found it amazing that she managed to say the words without even flinching; as though it didn't even bother her.

How could a woman know that their man was going to lay, kiss and have sex with another woman, and then come back home to do the same thing to them, and it not bother them?

How could any woman simply lay there while her mate *pumped* on top of her, knowing that he had just come from *pumping* on top of someone else, and she not even care?

The whole thing baffled me.

But that was her relationship and her problem.

Once we were inside the club, we headed to the bar and patiently waited for the bartender to get us our drinks.

"Ten o'clock," Delilah whispered and nodded over my shoulder at the man standing right behind me.

Slowly, I turned around to see a tall, dark chocolate fellow staring at me as if I was a piece of meat on a stick.

He smiled at the sight of my face and I damn near threw up at the sight of his teeth.

Oh hell no!

His teeth didn't have a stitch of white on them. They were stained a dirty, dark brown that even in a club setting, was noticeable. And they were crisscrossed, crooked and everything else.

Either he couldn't afford the proper dental work, didn't have a job that came with insurance, or he didn't care enough about himself to keep up with the maintenance of his hygiene and routine necessary dental exams.

Either way, he had better get the hell out of my face!

I turned back around, hurriedly, and ignored his taps on my shoulder until we got our drinks.

I walked off without even looking back at him and as soon as we were far enough away from him, the girls burst into laughter and began to tease.

What was he thinking?

I would have never been able to look at him, let alone let him put his mouth on me.

There was a woman somewhere that probably wouldn't mind his teeth, but I wasn't her.

My future mate at least had to be able to smile at me without making me sick to my stomach.

I simply shook my head and realized that I only came out to waste time and to get out of the house.

The type of man that I wanted wasn't going to be found here. The type of man that I wanted most likely wouldn't be found in a club.

So, what the hell was I even doing here?

The girls sat their drinks down on the table in front of us and headed to the dance floor.

I took a seat in one of the chairs and sipped on my mixed drink.

I smiled at them as they danced and motioned for me to come and join them, but I declined.

I immediately wished that I had driven.

I would have probably gotten up and left. I could think of a hundred other things that I'd rather be doing at that moment.

But since I was riding shotgun, I was stuck.

And from the looks of it, the girls wouldn't want to leave anytime soon.

I guess if I got too bored, I could always call a cab.

The drink was delicious and soothing and as I nodded to the beat of the music, I closed my eyes to focus on the words.

They sure don't make music the way that they used to, I tell you that much. I had no idea what it was that the singer was talking about.

I was sure that it had something to do with money and ass but I wasn't familiar with the slang words that they were using.

But the beat reminded me of an old school jam.

I absolutely loved music.

Coming up, I'd only heard gospel music, but my college roommate introduced me to the soothing sounds of rhythm and blues and everything from the 80's and 90's.

From then on, music was my escape.

It my medicine when I was sick. It my therapy when I was feeling low.

Music was love.

And I loved me some music!

At the sound of commotion, I opened my eyes to see Donna's boyfriend in the face of the man that she had been dancing with.

My heart skipped at a beat as Donna jumped in between them and tried to control her mate but by then the other guy was a live wire.

It all happened so fast and before I knew it, shots were fired and I was on the floor underneath the table.

I was too afraid to look up so I simply laid there, covering my head for a long while until someone touched my back.

I looked behind me and it was the man from the bar with the messed up teeth. He reached for my hand and cautiously, I took it.

On my feet, I looked in the direction where the altercation had begun and I covered my mouth at the sight of not only Donna but also Delilah lying on the floor.

I tried to head in their direction, but the stranger grabbed me and pushed me toward the exit instead.

Lord please let them be okay.

***

"How are you holding up?" I asked Delilah.

She was now home from the hospital.

Through all of the gun fire, she'd been hit in the shoulder by a stray bullet.

Unfortunately Donna, her man, the guy she was dancing with and one other person, had been pronounced dead at the scene.

It had all happened so quickly that it still seemed unreal.

I couldn't believe that it had escalated to something that turned deadly.

The whole ordeal was definitely confirmation as to how unhealthy relationships could cost you not only your self-respect and dignity, but you could be one of the many that it actually cost you your life.

Delilah was still in a state of shock, so I was over at her place helping her and tending after my god child.

"I still can't believe that she's gone," Delilah said softly as she laid her head on my shoulder.

"She was the only *real* friend that I'd ever had."

I don't know why her words stung my heart like a thousand bees but it did.

I wanted to say...

Well bitch what am I?

Even though she had some jealousy towards me and underlying issues, I had been nothing but a good friend to her.

But the truth was to truth, no matter how well you tried to hide it. And now that I knew the truth, instead of just assuming, I could now embrace and deal with it accordingly.

"Everything is going to be okay," I said to her and rubbed her back.

"No it won't. She wasn't supposed to die. Now, I'll never be able to tell her that I'm sorry for sleeping with Big Ox."

Big Ox is what they called Donna's baby's father on the street.

As soon as she'd said the words, I glanced at Bryson, my god son, and took a good look at him, just to make sure that he didn't resemble him.

Thankfully he didn't.

Hell, you just never know with whores.

And that was the only way to describe Delilah after what she'd just confessed.

I would have killed to have seen the outcome of Delilah breaking the news to Donna.

I could only imagine that Donna would have given her the beat down that she very much deserved.

Delilah should be ashamed of herself.

There are just some things that you just don't do. There are just some lines that you just don't cross.

I sat with them for a little while longer before making my exit.

Delilah would be out of work for the next week or two so I vowed to come by and check on the two of them every few days.

I could have offered to take the Bryson with me but unlike her, I still had to be at work the next day and of course I had no one to help me look after him.

Pulling off, I thought about how disrespectful and untrustworthy Delilah truly was.

I mean really, sleeping with her best friend's man?

Hell, if she would do that to her best friend, there's no telling what she would do to me.

I mean what was she thinking?
Even If he approached her, she shouldn't have ever opened her legs to him.

I never understood how a woman could lay with a man that was already lying with someone else.

There's no way in hell that I would want a penis that I knew first hand that it had been in any relative's or friend's mouth or in her *secret purse.*

Ugh, I just don't understand.

But I was a virgin for a reason, so I guess maybe I wasn't supposed to.

But right was right and wrong was wrong.

At what point do your morals kick in when you're doing something like that to someone that you say that you love?

I didn't have all of the answers, but I did have the truth.

The truth was that Delilah couldn't be trusted.

The *spilling of her beans*, confirmed that Delilah was a friend to no one.

And you know what?

She was definitely not a friend that I wanted or needed in my space, not even if it was for *pretend.*

I loved little Bryson, I really did, but maybe she was going to have to find him a new god mommy.

The truth to the matter was that I pretty much had zero tolerance for bull crap.

But then again, that was clear.

On another subject, I will say this though, life is too short.

Feelings of fulfillment were definitely at an all-time high considering what had happened to Donna and what could have happened to Delilah.

So, needless to say, it was past time for me to start enjoying the pleasures of life rather than working myself to death.

It was definitely an eye opener, and I was sure that Donna's funeral was going to make it even clearer that the time for me to start living was now.

It was so easy to be alive but there were tons of people, including me, who weren't actually living.

It was time for me to loosen up and just start living.

I had never gotten around to calling my mother, and since it was a Sunday, I decided to head on over to the hospital.

She too could be gone in an instant, and I needed to do better with spending time with her and showing her how much I loved her, even though we had some issues.

Walking into the facility, I always got this eerie feeling and always felt as though my mother really didn't belong there.

Sure, she had done some strange things throughout the years such as grabbing a baby from a woman's arms and running down the street with the baby because she'd said she could see *demons* in them.

She'd done that, along with a few other things, all linking to religion, but still yet, in my opinion, she wasn't exactly *crazy*.

Who am I to say that she didn't really see some of those things?

Coming up in the church, I'd learned to be more than optimistic, but society wasn't as accepting of some of the things that my mother had done as a result of her religious beliefs.

But still to this day, I blamed my father for my mother's condition or behavior.

The broken heart that he'd caused her is what had made her the way that she was today.

As she walked in my direction, she was nothing like the woman that I remembered.

My mother had been a god-fearing woman that was so full of life, love and scriptures of course.

Though she was saved, she wasn't at all a bad parent. Of course in our opinion she went a little over board with teaching us the Gospel, but other than that, she took good care of us.

Our personal relationship was a little weird.

For some reason she didn't communicate with me as much or as freely as she did with my other siblings. I'd imagined that it was because I was so much like her.

I looked the most like her. I had her personality and I even smiled like her, but for some reason our connection just wasn't as strong.

Naturally, I felt some kind of disconnection with or towards her, but I still loved her with everything in me.

She was my mother; the only one that I'd been given and she could never be replaced.

"Hey mama," I said to her as we sat down at one of the tables in the visiting area.

"You look good Tori. Thanks for coming to visit me," she said.

I was surprised that she knew who I was.

I was shocked that she seemed to be in her right mind, and apparently it showed all over my face.

"I stopped taking the medicine. It was making my forgetful."

I smiled at her.

I was glad that she wasn't taking it, she didn't need it. But I at least wanted her to have a voice of reason.

"Are you sure Mama?"

"Tori, I'm not sick. And I'm not crazy. I never have been. What your father did to me was something bigger than a broken heart. It shook the foundation that I lived and breathed on and I felt as though God had failed me in some way. So, instead of turning from him, I went searching for deeper validation and I allowed the religion and everything in that Bible to control and consume me. I guess I did come off as a little bit crazy. But I'm not crazy," she said.

Her words brought tears to my eyes.

I wanted to hug her but I didn't want to make her feel uncomfortable.

"So, what do you want me to do? Get you out of here?"

"No, I'm fine here. I don't have anything to go back to out there. God can use me wherever I am. Don't worry about me, I'll be fine. So what's new with you?"

The sad part about it was that I didn't have anything new to tell her.

I really need to get a life.

***

"Maybe you should lower your standards a little bit," Delilah was trying to give me advice on dating as though I was going to listen to anything that she said.

It was the day after Donna's funeral and I was visiting them for the last time.

Delilah had decided to move back to Louisiana with her folks after the whole incident.

From what Delilah had told me, she and Donna had come to Washington together and now that Donna was gone, and because she didn't have any family here, there was no real reason for her to stay.

The funeral was beautiful.

It was a double funeral for Donna and Big Ox.

I'd never been to one like that before, but it turned out to be nice.

I'd cried like a newborn baby at the sight of Donna, lying there in her pearl-colored casket.

She looked so lovely and so at peace.

All I could seem to think about was that it could have been me.

One of those stray bullets could have had my name on it and I could have been gone just like that.

And what would I have truly done while I was here? Other than my educational and career accomplishments, if you took all of that away, what was left?

Looking at her two babies that day on the front pew definitely melted my heart. They were weeping for their mother and father, but they couldn't hear their cries.

I left the funeral changed forever in the inside.

I was going to make the most of my life from that day forward.

Delilah and I of course, promised to keep in touch, but I knew that that wasn't going to happen.

The most that I was going to do was send cards with money for little Bryson on birthdays and Christmas's but other than that, this was the end of the road for us.

She and her disloyalty didn't have a place in my life as I looked towards the future.

Leaving her house for the last time, I headed outside with a smile on my face.

The breeze was cool and for some reason, I was feeling like a brand new woman.

I felt as though I was ready for whatever and for starters it was time for me to find myself a man.

A real one.

I just had to figure out where to start.

What if all men came with a warning label? Wouldn't it make it a lot easier for us women to make better decisions with who we gave our hearts to?

But on the flip side, would women even take the time to actually read the label?

Or would they simply ignore it in hopes that the label was wrong?

I tell you one thing, and I can only speak for myself, and I would read the hell out of it.

Anything that would save me time and energy from dealing with the wrong guy was definitely worth reading.

But I was doing pretty darn good paying attention to the signs even without the physical labels.

Still in my thoughts, I walked to my car slowly, ignoring the whistling behind me.

What on earth would make a man think that any woman, in her *right* mind, would show them any kind of attention while they were whistling at her like she was a dog?

I guess it worked for some but it definitely didn't work for a woman like me.

I got into my car and drove away in a hurry.

Lower my standards my ass!

I was just going to find someone that met them. He was out there, and he was bound to be found.

Life was too short, and this woman was now on a mission.

****

Chapter Three

"I have someone for you. Let me set you up on a date," my boss, Hunter, said as he popped his head into my office.

I eyed him questionably.

There was no way in hell that I was going to take a dating recommendation from a lying, cheating scumbag like himself.

I still believed in the saying that birds of a feather flock together, so as far as I was concerned, everybody that was a friend, acquaintance, associate, or whatever of his were liars and cheaters just like he was.

And I wasn't going to take any chances.

I declined his offer with a smile and after pretending to listen to his point of view for about five minutes or so, finally went on his merry little way.

I sat staring at my computer and wondered if it was past time to explore the option of online dating.

After clicking on a few of the sites, I decided that I was too fine and too fly to have to go that route.

Tori, what is going on with you?

My conscious started to speak up.

Though the shooting incident had given me a reality check, and though I was a bit on edge about life being too short and I, I knew that it was risky to be in such a rush for love.

I had to calm down about it and get my mind together on the matter.

Everyone knows that patience is a virtue and that slow and steady always wins the race.

It will happen when it's supposed to happen.

So for now, I needed to get myself together for the twenty plus interviews up ahead for a new assistant.

Here goes nothing...

With one more interview to go, I glanced at my watch.

They only had about ten minutes to get there and if they were going to be late, they may as well not even show up.

Honestly, I preferred an assistant that was always a little bit early.

Delilah hadn't been much of a friend, but she had the assistant thing down to the tee.

She'd always done an amazing job, and she was going to be hard to replace.

A backstabbing, disloyal floozy with a good work ethic; now, that was something that you don't see every day!

Just as the thoughts crossed my mind, in walks this coffee-colored *stallion* of a man.

Whose man is he and why on earth couldn't he be mine?

"Hello, I'm Tristan Hall. I'm here for the interview."

Really?

There was no way that he was here to interview for the assistant position.

If anything he needed to be interviewing to be my husband, boyfriend, *boo-thang*...hell anything that included him, plus me, would suffice.

"Am I in the right place?"

I simply nodded my head, unable to speak.

So let me explain what was standing in front of me.

Height guess, I would say right at six feet.

Through his impressive choice of shirt and bow tie, I could see that his body was in tip top shape.

I was positive that he had abs and everything.

And those broad masculine shoulders and big arms had a *sista'* mesmerized beyond belief. I wondered if he had tattoos and how many.

Would it be extremely inappropriate to ask him to do the interview with his shirt off?

Yeah, okay, so maybe it would be.

But his body was all of that and then some.

Oh, and that smile...I won't even go there.

As he invited himself to take a seat in the chair across from my desk, I continued to study him.

His attire, nor did his appearance give off the impression that he was unemployed; so why was he here?

"Look, I'm an honest type of guy so I'm going to keep it real with you. I know this job is for an assistant, but actually I'm here for your job...well, at least one like it."

I smirked at his cockiness.

He didn't stand a chance at getting my position, but I liked his enthusiasm.

I didn't respond to him, I simply glanced down at his résumé.

If I had read it before hand, I would have seen that he wasn't unemployed, and that he already worked in Accounting.

"So, I see you already have a job in Accounting as well. Why leave your position to come and be my assistant? That's sort of a backwards step don't you think?"

"I've been trying to get in the door with you guys for years. So, I figured that if an assistant is the only thing that this company was hiring for, if I could get my foot in the door, I'm sure that I could seek the position that I truly desired."

A man with a plan...I like it.

As I said, we were the best in all of Washington and I wouldn't doubt that we were amongst the top ranked in the world.

If you needed accounting services or anything to do with money and if you were of a certain status...you came to us.

It was no question.

And as he stated, we rarely hired for any top executive or high level positions being that usually people that came never left and also we promoted a lot from within our company, versus bringing in someone new off of the street.

Basically, coming in as an assistant, cleaning crew or something like that was the best way and almost the only way for someone new to get through these doors these days.

But I just couldn't allow him to be my assistant.

Not only because I wouldn't be able to get any work done from gawking at and drooling over him all day, but he was definitely over qualified.

His qualifications, some of them, were indeed better than my own. I simply couldn't allow him to come in and do my light work.

But there was something that I *could* do.

"So, I'm going to be honest with you, I simply can't hire you as an assistant. It just wouldn't be right. But I do know that we have a position coming open in a couple of weeks that you would qualify for. One of our top executives will be retiring soon and of course someone will move into his spot, which means that someone will need to fill the successor's position. Now, usually we promote from within, but there are a couple of folks that owe me a few favors around this place. So, I could hold on to your résumé and see what I can do," I said to him.

He looked at me as if he was trying to decide whether or not he should believe that I would actually put in a good word for him.

I stared deep into his eyes to let him know that I meant business, and to also let him know that I was game for mixing a little business with pleasure.

As a matter of fact, it could be all pleasure.

Screw the business.

But he was here for a job, not a *blow* job; though I couldn't wait until the day that I was able to try one.

I'd watched enough examples and in my head I was already a pro.

He would be the perfect test-dummy for the *job.*

Tori, get your mind out of the gutter and pay attention, I internally scolded myself.

"Cool. Thank you and hopefully they pay up on a few of those favors that they owe you...or I'll be back," he smiled.

He stood up, tugged on his bow tie, and extended his hand for me to shake it.

Standing to my feet, I watched him as he appraised my body while he shook my hand for a second too long.

See, he just had to have a look...he was in trouble now!

As I said, I had the whole sexy thing down to the tee and just one glance was usually all it took for a man to what to know more.

I sure hoped this one did.

We smiled at each other and then he turned to walk away.

A little disappointed, I wanted to say something but I didn't know what to say.

I was full of words but at that moment, nothing and I mean absolutely nothing, would come out of my mouth.

Luckily, he decided to say something instead.

"So, since I didn't get the job...can I get your number?"

Before I could even answer him, he reached me his phone and I couldn't enter my number fast enough.

Yes! There is a God!

***

"Uh oh, I know that look," my oldest sister Cheyanne said to me, with a grin on her face.

I rolled my eyes and continued to shop as she and her three kids followed behind me.

Cheyanne was the oldest child of my parents' children and the one that I kind of saw as a mother figure.

She was the one that I'd always confided in and the one that I'd always looked to for advice.

Even before our mother was deemed as *sick*, Cheyanne was the one that I looked up to.

She was always the fun one. She was the dare devil of the bunch and the one who taught me that rules were sometimes made to be broken.

She was definitely a little on the wild side, but she'd calmed down as she'd gotten older. She was still a ball of fun to be around though.

Though she was well-educated, Cheyanne was now a stay at home mother of three and married to an ordinary, hard-working guy that was born and raised in South Carolina.

You could definitely tell that he was raised in the South, but he brought a nice Southern blend to our family.

My sister's husband was so *country* that you often caught him outside with no shoes on, and he always had my sister cooking things like neck-bones, cornbread or pigs feet.

From what I could see, she and my brother-in-law were pretty happy.

I wasn't around them as often as I wanted to be but believe me when I said that every time that I was I watched him, studied him, for signs of infidelity, just to see if I saw anything that might hint that he wasn't as happy as he portrayed to be.

To date, I'd never seen a thing, at least not on his end anyway.

My sister was the one that he needed to keep his eye on.

I'm just saying---she had a few *tendencies.*

Though she'd never mentioned anything, I was sure that she'd stepped out of the marriage once or twice or at least she wanted to.

"His name is Tristan."

"Um, that's it? That's all you have to say about him? You know that you are the queen of trying to figure a man out before he even says *hello,* so I'm sure there is something else that you have to say about him than just quoting his name," my sister quizzed.

I simply smiled at her and continued looking at the blouses that were in my hand.

The truth was that I didn't know what to think about Tristan.

I couldn't seem to figure him out, at least not yet anyway.

We'd only been talking for a few days, but so far he had been saying all of the right things.

He'd called only about ten minutes after he'd left my office. His reasoning was that he wanted to make sure that I had given him the right number.

He'd said that women today were known to give a man the wrong *digits* just so that they could avoid the extra of turning them down.

I liked that he was up front, aggressive and honest. He didn't bite his tongue and he said exactly what was on his mind.

It was refreshingly intriguing.

Since that day, we talked regularly.

Well, regularly was an understatement.

We talked all the time!

I rarely had to call him because he made sure that he called me. He called me as if we'd been dating for months, and I answered every single time.

The amount of free time that he on his hands told me that he didn't have too many *attachments.*

It showed that he had lots of time to spare and give to me.

He was my type of man already.

I have to admit, I wasn't used to all of the attention and it was more than flattering.

He complemented me every chance that he got and sad some of the sweetest things that I'd ever heard.

And it was making it hard for me to have a clear head and pay attention to every little thing that he said and did.

Just a little bit.

But still yet, though it wasn't as easy, I had my eyes open.

I was looking for the signs.

I knew that eventually something would begin to show if there was something for me to see.

I only hoped and prayed that he was as wonderful as he appeared to be.

Considering that we both worked quite a bit and that sometimes it was necessary to pull a few extra hours, finally, we were scheduled to go on our first date, soon, and I was really looking forward to it.

I wanted to see him in a different environment and in a different light.

"Tori?"

"What Cheyanne? I don't want to jinx anything so for now all you need to know is that his name is Tristan," I laughed as she rolled her eyes.

Speaking again of Mr. Tristan, I decided that I was going to give him a call.

Since he'd always called first, I hadn't been able to see how he would react or what he would be doing if I decided to give him an unexpected *ring*.

In my opinion, and because previous experiences have always proven me right, if a man can calls you, but *never* answers when you call him, the truth is...he probably has a lady.

Even if he calls you back soon after, but is either outside or always riding in a car, or even is bold enough to answer and give you a few quick words before he says that he will call you back...again...he's probably already taken.

I'm telling you what I know to be true.

Granted this may not be true in every, single case or with every single man.

He could simply just be busy.

He could have been asleep or in the shower or even outside mowing the lawn.

But if it's something that repeatedly happens, then a year's salary says that something isn't what he says that it is.

I was willing to bet on it.

I'd been down that road enough times to know.

And no, all men aren't the same, but I'm just saying:

Pay attention to the signs...or pay the consequences later.

So, here goes nothing, I thought.

The phone ranged three times and as the forth ring started to come in, my finger headed to the end button. But just as I pulled the phone away from my ear, I heard his voice.

"Hello!" Tristan screamed.

"I'm sorry, are you busy?" I asked him, already expecting him to say yes.

"Nope. I was getting me a work out in but since you called, I'm done," Tristan said and I could tell that he was smiling.

Okay, so, not what I expected.

Now, I had to figure out something else to say.

We small talked for a while longer and decided to see each other that night for a movie, instead of waiting for our planned date night that next Wednesday.

He said that he couldn't wait to see me and that he was tired of staring at the pictures of me in his phone that I'd sent him.

Hanging up the phone, I texted him my address and then I turned around to face my sister.

"Oh my, you're blushing. Okay, can we talking about who Tristan is now?" she asked as I started to giggle.

After hanging out with my sister and the kids a little while longer, I headed home to find a bear and a single balloon on my front porch.

There was a note pinned to the bear's chest that said:

I can Bear-ly not (barely) wait to see you tonight.
Tristan.

Aww, how sweet!

I was definitely blushing as I sniffed the bear for his scent and then carried it and the balloon inside the house.

He must have come by and left the surprise no sooner than I'd sent him my address.

I text him to say thank you, and he immediately responded saying that I deserved it.

This man was definitely trying to sweep me off of my feet and I was enjoying every minute of it.

It had been a long time that I'd had someone that was even half as charming as he was.

To think of it, there was one that might have given him a run for his money, but he turned out to be a little more aggressive than I was willing to deal with.

Mason was his name.

He was a professor and I just loved to listen to him speak.

It seemed as though every time that I was in his presence I learned something new. He was always saying something sweet or reciting poetry.

He always took the time to do something nice for me and I was more than appreciative of it.

But I soon found out that if something didn't exactly go his way, things could get very ugly...including my face.

One day, after a slight disagreement, right in public, he'd reached across the table and smacked me.

To this day, I'm banned from that restaurant, we both were.

We tore that place down!

Luckily, he was the one that ended up going to jail and the police let me go, considering that he had been the one to imitate the fight.

He was crazy to think that I was going to let him put his hands on me without retaliating.

He called me the next day begging for my forgiveness, saying that he was stressed and so on and so forth but God himself would have had to come down off of the throne in Heaven, to tell me to give him another chance.

There was just no way in Hell that I would ever let him close to me again.

I'd seen what I'd needed to see and a woman beater label was forever stamped to his chest.

That life just wasn't for me.

I stopped reminiscing and headed to my bedroom to prepare to get dressed.

We were only going to a movie, so there was no need to overdress, but I still wanted to look cute.

I found the perfect outfit and headed to get myself together.

I couldn't believe that I actually had a date.

It had been a long time and I only hoped that things turned out okay.

Well, we shall see...

"You look amazing *woman*," Tristan chuckled as I stepped out of my front door.

I usually didn't allow men to come to my house on the first date, but for Tristan, I'd made an exception.

I looked at his attire.

Though we were only going to a movie, he was impeccably dressed from head to toe.

"You look amazing yourself...*man*," I chimed as he opened the passenger side door of his Mustang.

His car choice actually surprised me.

I hadn't taken him for a Mustang type of guy but more so an Audi, or maybe a Volvo if not the high named brands such as Mercedes and a few others.

It wasn't even an up to date Mustang, but it was new enough and it was clean and it smelled good.

Maybe he had another car too, I concluded.

Even if he didn't, I guess the fact that he had a decent car was all that mattered, for now anyway.

I was surprised at the fact that I wasn't being as judgmental as usual.

Maybe I was trying to be a little more open minded or maybe it was that I just didn't want to mess something up before it had even begun.

Hell or maybe it was just that secretly and in the deepest part of my heart, I was just tired of being alone.

Whatever the reason was, it was time for me to snag a man and hold on to him.

And Tristan was definitely a man worth snagging.

He entered the car and turned up the radio.

I was surprised to hear that he was listening to old school.

I loved my old school!

I guess again I'd assumed incorrectly.

I'd imagined him being one to listen to jazz or classical music but the way that he sung every word to the tune that was playing, told me that it was way past time for me to stop making assumptions about him.

My grandmother used to say that assuming would make an ass out of you and me.

Get it?

Ass-u-me...assume.

I guess I was imagining him to do, say, drive and be the man of my dreams but I had to start living in my reality.

And the reality was that no man was going to have everything on my list, so I had better start bending or I was going to be alone and in trouble in the long run.

Yes, a Mustang, I could deal with.

Old school music was the best that there was.

Now, if it had been rap music, I'm not so sure. Nothing against it, and I even listened to it here and there, but let's just say that with the kind of rap music that was out today, I definitely didn't want a man that constantly polluted his mind with that nonsense.

Sorry, that's just my preference.

But then again, at this moment, Tristan could have been listening to rap, country and whatever else, as long as I could be in his presence.

He took one hand off of the steering wheel and placed it on my lap for me to grab it.

I felt like a teenage girl on her first date.

Only that I hadn't had the pleasure of experiencing a first date in my early teen years.

Of course that was due to the way that we were raised and because my parents' were so religious.

They were convinced that if a boy even sneezed in any of our direction, we would get pregnant.

To be honest, I was so afraid of the things that they'd said, I'd become accustom to not even looking at or paying boys my age much attention at all.

So, I didn't have my first real date until I was a sophomore in college.

My first date had been with a man named Pablo.

He was Hispanic and black and he was about ten years older than I was at the time.

I'd met him while waitressing part-time.

The church scholarship covered my tuition and living arrangements, but anything else I wanted, I had to work for it.

Anyway, he was a regular customer and tipped me fairly well every time that he came to the restaurant. One day, along with the tip, he gave me his phone number.

I was young then, and even though I had an eye for spotting *bull*, I wasn't an expert just yet.

The obvious signs were all there but I missed them until it was too late.

The first time I called him, I can remember getting his voicemail and when I tried two other times that same day, I hadn't gotten a response then either.

Finally, early the next day, he called and gave me some crazy excuse and basically gave me times that it was best to call him.

At the time, I figured that it was all innocent since he was a car salesman and his hours were all over the place, but really it was because he had a full plate.

After communicating for a few days over the phone, he asked to take me out on one of my days off.

Granted I was younger, I was smart.

And I had already had an idea of the type of man that I wanted. I thought for maybe a second that he could have been just my type, but I had been so wrong.

The date itself was fine and memorable.

He took me to a five star restaurant, bought me roses, and even looked into my eyes and told me everything that a girl wanted to hear.

I felt special, and the attention actually felt good but walking out of that restaurant to see that man's wife and her best friend, standing there at his car, waiting for us, told me that I had to be more careful and pay closer attention.

Needless to say, he didn't even try to help me fight them off.

They jumped me and he just stood there, yelling at his wife as we went toe to toe.

I didn't go down without a fight though.

I fought both of those grown ass women with everything that I had in me. Had I not fallen, maybe the outcome would have been different, but since I did, I ended up with a broken nose and a few fractured ribs.

The sad part about it all was that I was innocent.

I wasn't the one at fault.

I truly didn't know about her or even that he was married since he didn't wear a wedding ring, but I, as well as my health insurance, ended up paying the price.

Assuming that she'd finally paid attention to him constantly yelling that I didn't know that he was married, finally she stopped and called off her best friend.

I laid there on the pavement for a while in pain as they argued about his lying and cheating ways.

Finally, he helped me to his car, drove me to the hospital in silence, and dropped me off.

That was it.

No apology, not one single word.

The police were called and when attempting to press charges, the number that I had for him actually belonged to one of his buddies, who allowed him to call me from it when he was around.

That explained why he only answered if I called at the times that he'd given me. I guess that was when he was around him.

Anyway, the friend pretty much covered for him and pretended not to know where he was.

I didn't know the exact car dealership that he worked at and I quickly found out that Pablo wasn't even his real name.

I simply decided to just let it all go and count it as a lesson learned.

That was when I vowed to never let something like that happen to me again.

No, men didn't come with printed labels stamped to their foreheads, but if you paid close attention, you could spot the invisible warning label, sitting, waiting on you to read its content.

And now, I always paid attention.

The car came to a halt and I shook away the thoughts of my past and waited for him to open my door.

I smiled at him but took a quick second to silently say a prayer.

Lord, whatever it may be, make sure you send me a sign....

The movie was good---at least I assumed it was.

To be honest, I hadn't watched hardly any of it. I was too busy entertaining my thoughts about Tristan.

I liked the way he smelled and the way that he firmly held my hand. I liked the way that he sat with his knees far apart as though he had something large and powerful tucked away between his muscular thighs.

I even liked the way that he breathed.

Everything about him just made me want to do something to him...something that I could only hope that he would like.

I know, I was still a virgin, but I'd watched a good amount of porn. I was sure that I was going to be ready whenever the time arrived.

But for now, I was enjoying imagining what sex would be like with the man that was by my side.

We arrived at my place shortly after and I was almost sad that the night was about to end.

I'd already shared with him up front that I was saving myself for true love and he'd understood, but in a way I'd wished that I hadn't said anything to him at all.

I know I was waiting for the right guy, but what if he never came?

Then what?

And if my first time wasn't with the *right* guy, it might as well have been with a guy like Tristan.

Yet, I hid my frustrations with a smile and nearly ran into the house once he kissed me goodnight.

I couldn't make it to my room fast enough as I opened my top drawer and grabbed my Bo.

Yeah, after tonight, I was definitely going to need some new batteries.

***

I hadn't spoken to Delilah since she'd left and just my luck she was calling just as I was getting dressed for date number two with Tristan.

I sent her to my voicemail and continued getting dressed.

Yes, in a way, I missed her.

I would be lying if I said that I didn't.

But I knew that her moving away was the best thing for the both of us.

I needed and wanted real and genuine people in my life and I rather not entertain anyone less than.

I stared at myself in the full length mirror.

Yet again, I wanted to be sexy, but not too sexy. I wanted to be teasingly attractive and not just to Tristan; but to any other man that would lay his eyes on me tonight.

The truth is, no man wants what other man don't want so, I was hoping to get a few stares from by standers, to allow Tristan to get the big picture.

He would have a diamond on his arm tonight and diamonds weren't just a woman's best friend.

Men better act like they know!

Just as I finished the last few touches of my makeup, Tristan was calling to say that he'd arrived.

I glanced at myself one last time, took a deep breath, and rushed out the front door.

Tonight was going to be amazing!

The conversation as we drove was different than usual.

Though he had always been open and honest, tonight he was being funny and showing a lot of his intelligence.

He was so freaking attractive!

From his appearance to his mind, he just continued to impress me. And I hadn't been impressed by a man in a very long time.

We walked into a restaurant that I had never heard of but from the looks of it, it was loved and quite popular.

It was overly crowed and people were holding buzzers, waiting for an open table but luckily Tristan had reservations for us.

The waitress led us to our table and Tristan pulled out my chair.

I love the fact that he was showing all of the signs of a gentleman. That was a good thing.

My father had been the idea of the perfect gentleman...minus the whole mistress thing.

But coming up, I had seen him open doors, pull out chairs, and stand up whenever my mother left the table, the whole nine yards.

He'd taught my brother's to do the same thing and it was just something that I'd become accustom to seeing.

So, a gentleman was definitely something that was on my list and just one of those things that I wasn't going to let slide.

"Order whatever you'd like or do you trust me to order for you?" Tristan said somewhat sure but still with a touch of sarcasm.

He was definitely a take charge type of man and I had to admit, it turned me on.

I liked the thought that he could handle me and take charge of me even though a lot of men found me intimidating.

But Tristan didn't seem scared of me or challenged by me at all.

Though I didn't particularly trust his choice in food, at least not just yet, I allowed him to order for me anyway.

We were at an Italian restaurant if I wasn't mistaken and I was excited to try new foods.

After I tried something new, I always tried to mimic the recipe and usually ended up creating something that tasted a lot better, so I was ready to give a few things a try.

"Taste this," Tristan ordered once our food was placed in front of us.

It was a soup called Zuppa di Pesce and I was in love after just one bite.

"It's good huh?"

I couldn't say a thing, so I just nodded my head.

From there, the entire dinner went by with a breeze and everything about the night was incredible.

I had to force myself to come off of cloud nine for a while just to watch his every move and pay attention to everything that he said.

I was looking for something, anything that might raise an eyebrow but from the looks of it, there was nothing to see.

And then it hit me.

Maybe this was it.

Maybe this was him.

The man that I'd waited my entire life for.

The man that no one said exists.

I'd had my share of liars, cheaters, broke men and even a deadbeat father or two, and maybe now, was my time to get the man that I actually deserved.

I smiled.

My Boaz had found me after all.

****

Chapter Four

"I passed your information on to my associate. Don't be surprised if you hear from someone soon for an interview," I said to Tristan, just shy of a whisper.

We were at my place, cuddling on the couch watching television.

For the past two months and a half, we'd been inseparable.

When neither of us was working, we were always with each other.

We were getting to know each other more and more each day and we had a connection that was very different from anything that I'd ever experienced.

From being around him, not only was I learning him, but I was learning a few things about myself that I hadn't noticed or paid much attention to before.

Now, things weren't as perfect or peachy as they had been in the beginning.

I'd seen a few things that I wasn't too fond of pertaining to Tristan, but they weren't major things.

They weren't deal breakers.

I mean, they truly were really small things.

For instance, I was a neat freak and here lately I learned that it may have been a little more serious than just being neat, maybe it was boarder line OCD but as for Tristan...he was not.

His name and neat shouldn't even be allowed to be in the same sentence.

There were times where I felt like I was picking up after a five year old.

He just seemed to do most things, so sloppy and that's if he'd bothered to do them at all.

I refused to stay over at his house because I could only imagine what it looked like in the inside.

I had only been outside of it a few times, while he ran inside for a change of clothes.

It was cute, not particularly my taste, but cute. I could only imagine how messy it probably was and I didn't want to see anything that I couldn't force myself to forget.

So, I always declined his offer to stay over and would suggest that we stayed at my house instead.

I'd built my house from the ground up.

It was just the way that I wanted it.

It was cozy, stunning; it was perfect.

I'd built it on a wing and a prayer that I would one day have enough *rug-rats* to fill it.

I was laughed at for building the house first.

I'd been told that I should at least be married or to wait and see what my future husband brought to the table, but I couldn't wait around for something that I didn't know when or if it was going to happen.

So, I built my dream home and it was the nicest house on the block too.

Tristan often complimented me on its beauty, even though he was steadily making it look a hot mess.

Cleaning house from top to bottom had been the normal for me since I was a small child, and I was disappointed that he hadn't been taught to do the same.

I couldn't stand a nasty home.

A nasty house made my ass itch.

To think of it, Delilah had been borderline nasty and her house was never truly cleaned. I used to hate to even sit on her couch and often stood unless I was going to be there for a long time.

I just couldn't deal with it.

And I surely wasn't going to deal with it in my own home, so Tristan had better get with the program.

Another thing that I wasn't particularly fond of when it came to Tristan was that I hadn't met any of his family as of yet.

To be honest, he never even talked about them.

And anytime I mentioned them, he let it be known that his family had never been there for him and that he'd rather not have a conversation about it.

The only thing that he'd shared was that his father had passed away a while ago and that his mother moved out of town soon after.

He only had one sibling, a younger brother who of course went with his mother after his father's death.

But that was about it.

Call me traditional, but a relationship was never truly a relationship until you've at least met the parents, hence is why I'd taken Tristan to visit Mama at the hospital.

She loved him too. I could tell.

She smiled at him and talked to him. I'd even had to make a quick run, but Tristan stayed and talked to her the whole time.

I was surprised with how well she communicated with him but she talked and talked to him as if she'd known him for years.

And though I could tell that Tristan had no idea what she was referring to half of the time, he always listened and responded.

He was the best!

Mama shared a few scriptures with him and he treated her with nothing but respect.

He was just the sweetest man alive and he'd earned my respect on a whole new level after the visit with my mother.

Meeting my mother was a success!

Of course I didn't have a father to take him home too. Usually, I told the men that I dated that my father was dead, but I actually told Tristan the truth.

Well, partially the truth.

I simply told him that I hadn't seen my father in years and that I didn't know if he was dead or alive.

And truthfully, I really didn't.

I didn't go into detail about anything else because he really didn't need to know anything but the obvious.

My father had abandoned us.

The end.

But other than those two small issues, the laziness and the lack of family mingling on his end, being with

Tristan was amazing and it was everything that I'd imagined love to be.

No, I wouldn't say that I was in love completely with him just yet.

But one day I was sure that I would.

I was definitely on my way.

Nevertheless, to my remarks about the job, Tristan simply nodded.

I did have some worries about us working in the same building and at the same firm.

It wasn't about competition or anything because though he was smart, he could never replace me.

That firm was nothing without me and my big money clients. I was sure that if I walked out and started my own firm that more than half of my clients would follow me, which meant that their money would follow me too.

But I did wonder if it would be too much on such a new relationship to be around each other all day, every day.

I mean not that we were in a real relationship, and then again, maybe we were.

I was sure that folks didn't still ask to be boyfriend and girlfriend these days, it just sort of happened.

And we had been sort of happening for quite some time now.

But no matter what we were, I didn't want it to affect my job or our relationship.

As Tristan dozed off, I eyed his phone that was vibrating on the table.

I know some say that they aren't the snooping type of chick...well, sorry, I am!

I will investigate and whatever else if it meant saving myself a headache or heartache.

I'll run a background check and all if I have enough pieces of information and a reason to do so.

Hey, sometimes it's the only way to get the truth. You gotta' do what you gotta' do these days.

As soon as Tristan lightly began to snore, I reached for his cell phone.

I was surprised to see that he didn't even have a lock on it.

Even I locked my phone and I only had a handful of people that called me.

Glancing at him one last time, I entered his text messages with caution.

And from there I checked his call logs and even had the nerve to press one to check his voicemail.

But after ten minutes of snooping, I came up with...nothing.

There wasn't a thing in his phone that was suspicious or out of place. Not one call that didn't seem normal and not one text message that even appeared to have been something other than what it was.

I was convinced.

This man was clean as a whistle.

Whew!

I guess I expected to see something that was going to make him wish that he'd never met me, but thankfully I had been wrong.

Every time it came to him, I was wrong.

I eased off of the couch, placing the phone back on the table and headed to the kitchen to cook dinner.

I had only cooked for him a few times so far, but he absolutely loved my cooking.

He said that my cooking reminded him of how his mama used to cook on Sundays, so I had some big shoes to continue to fill.

Today, I decided to make lasagna.

My siblings often joked that my lasagna was the reason that they had either gotten pregnant or gotten their wives pregnant.

They'd said that anytime that I made it, and they ate it, it gave them that extra kick to do something a little strange with their spouses that night afterwards and nine months later popped out the proof.

Baby-making in a pan is what they called it and I hoped that one day soon it would have the same magic effect on me.

"What's that smell?"

"It smells good don't it?"

"Yes it does. My mouth is watering," Tristan said as he approached me rubbing his eyes.

"Dinner is almost ready," I smiled as he planted a light kiss on my lips.

I looked at him as if I was asking him if he was kissing his grandma with my eyes.

He got the hint and chuckled.

He then kissed me again but this time it was a kiss that caused my *juices* to instantly begin to flow, drenching the insides of my thighs.

I attempted to move away from him but he grabbed me and pulled me close.

He'd made it very clear that he was only waiting for sex because it was important to me, but that didn't mean that he hadn't tried to tempt me every chance that he could.

I inched away from the stove until my back hit the island in the center of the kitchen.

In one swift motion, I was off of my feet and felt the coolness of the marble top against the back of my thighs.

His kisses became more aggressive and my body temperature started to heat up.

I felt excited yet scared all at the same time.

My *puss-pop* screamed yes, take me now, but my heart and mind warned me---not yet.

I was just going to kiss him.

That's it.

There was nothing wrong with a little kissing.

I reminded myself of my intentions as Tristan reached for my left breast.

I'd had my breasts sucked before, but not by Tristan and he was my weakness.

I was never sure of what I might do when I was around him and from the looks of it, things was about to get out of hand if I didn't put a stop to them now.

But I couldn't move. I could barely breathe.

I wanted to stop him, I really did, but I just couldn't.

As he placed his mouth around my nipple, the warmth of his tongue caused my *kitty* to purr.

My vagina had developed a heartbeat of *her* own and I had never experienced an arousal that was so intense in all of my life.

I felt Tristan's hand begin to roam over my thighs and then under my dress.

I felt him begin to tug on the edges of my panties.

I managed to say the word *stop*, but he wasn't listening, or maybe it was that he couldn't hear me.

Hell, I was confused, maybe I hadn't said the word at all because he continued to tug until his finger finally entered my *kitty-cat's mouth*.

I cooed as *she* spit her juices at his fingers by the gallons. I could feel him, swiftly moving his fingers, in and out of me, constantly harassing my clitoris.

The feeling was indescribable, so I didn't attempt to try to fight with him. I just continued to let him take me to the point of no return.

My mind was racing and I didn't know which felt better, the sucking or the fondling so I eagerly tried to enjoy both.

My mouth had started to moan without my permission and soon my moans turned into screams, yet Tristan remained diligently on task.

They say hard work pays off and it was time to pay him his dues for the services that he had rendered unto my *vagigi* and what better way to pay him than to show him the evidence of my satisfaction?

And that's exactly what I did.

Seconds later, I shared with him something that I had only shared with my *Bo*.

I released the *creams of my contentment* and Tristan finally spit out my breast.

As I tried to catch my breath, he smiled at me, slyly, as if he had just gotten away with murder.

"Well now that that's done and over with...let's eat," he said as he headed to the bathroom to wash his hands.

I shook my head and thought about what had just taken place.

I couldn't help but to smile and become excited about the fact that that was only the beginning of sexual exchanges between us.

I hopped off of the counter and headed behind him to the bathroom.

Until next time…and that time it wouldn't be his finger that was inside of me.

And I was for sure of that.

***

"Hi Hunter, what can I do for you?" I asked my peeping boss.

He was always somewhere watching, like some kind of predator.

I was actually surprised that he was still there. It was a lot later than he usually stayed.

"I was just coming by to one, tell you to go home…and that is an order. You're going to work yourself until you fall over and die. I told you I know the perfect man for you. But you won't let me *hook you up*, as you would say."

I cracked a smile at him but I didn't respond.

"Two, your referral never got back to Richard for an interview. Are they still interested in the job?"

I was surprised by his remark.

Tristan was darn near stalking his phone, day and night for that phone call.

"Are you sure that they called the right number? He has been waiting on that phone call for the past two weeks?"

"And how would you know that?" Hunter eyed me suspiciously.

Damn it...I said too much.

I had to think of something to say that would at least halfway sound convincing.

He didn't need to know my personal business.

"He called a few times. He wanted to know if I had kept my word and passed on his information. Hold on, let me see if I can find the number for him to make sure that Richard has the right one," I stated, pretending to be looking for a piece of paper as if I had taken down his number a time or two.

I didn't even bother to look up at Hunter.

"Tori, when you find it just email it to me and I will see to it that Richard gets it. And I was serious...go home," he said and turned his back to me.

He didn't have to tell me twice.

It was time for me to go home anyway because I was sure that Tristan was already there waiting for me.

I hadn't worked late in a while, until recently when I discovered that a few things were being missed on my end, probably as a result of always having my head up Tristan's ass.

But I was enjoying being in a relationship.

Yep, it was confirmed, I was in a relationship!

Ain't God good?

Things were still going well and I was extremely happy.

Things were going just fine between us and I wanted them to stay that way.

I gathered my things and waited for the night janitor to turn his head toward the window just as he always did to make sure that I made it to my car safely.

Safely inside, I decided that I didn't want to listen to any music on my way home.

I just wanted to ride in silence and gather my thoughts.

The first thing that crossed my mind was of course Tristan.

Who would have thought that I would have ended up with a man who came in to interview with me for a position?

Even I wasn't expecting the amount of joy that he had brought my way.

He was always doing nice things for me.

It felt good to receive flowers just because, or cards just to say how much I meant to him.

He washed my car, he washed my hair and other little things that would always make my day.

My days didn't seem as long.

My nights weren't half as lonely.

He wasn't perfect, but his love was mine and it was real. And the love that was growing for him, daily, was real also.

"I'm home," I smiled.

Of course I had given Tristan a key to my place.

It only made sense since usually he was off first, and was always outside waiting for my arrival.

He'd given me a key to his as well, but to date I'd never used it.

He was never there, he was always with me, and so I hadn't had to.

Tristan appeared in the hallway, coming from my bedroom.

He had a towel wrapped around his waist and he headed up the hallway towards me.

"How was your day?" he asked, kissing my cheek.

His body was still damp from the shower he must have just finished taking. I could smell the strong scent of *Irish Spring* seeping out from his pores.

My mouth started to water, so I cleared my throat.

"What's wrong baby?" Tristan asked coming closer.

The room seemed to grow smaller and smaller as he invaded my personal space.

The warmth of his breath harassed the hairs on my neck and my briefcase and purse, slipped from my hands and dropped to the floor.

Screw this whole virginity thing...it's time!

I allowed my body to tell him that I was ready, instead of using my words.

I had never ridden in this *rodeo* before, so I allowed Tristan to take the lead.

After light kissing and touching and removing all of my clothes, he took my hand and led me and my bare ass to the bedroom.

I was as nervous as a stripper in church, who was headed to the altar for some much need prayer.

I entered the bedroom to find candles all over the place as if he'd known that tonight was going to be the night.

I tried not to pay attention to how messy the room was.

At least he could have straighten up first before he'd tried to be romantic, but in an attempt to not ruin the moment, I focused on Tristan and his every move.

He led me to the bed and motioned for me to sit down. I took a deep breath and tried to relax.

This was the right decision.

I've never been more in tune with and attached to anyone else in my entire life.

Was it true love?

It definitely felt like it was going to be.

It had only been a few months, but this felt like the real thing.

Tristan was the real deal.

Tristan had voiced his feelings for me on several occasions and I knew for a fact that he was all in this and that the ball was in my court.

He showed me that he loved me on a daily basis, with everything that he did and everything that he said. He'd told me that never before had he considered settling down, until he met me.

I had to admit, I was feeling the exact same way.

So, with that being said, he'd earned the right to be my first...maybe even my last...and hopefully my only.

"Are you sure?" Tristan said as he got down on his knees in front of me.

Still, instead of speaking, I kissed him.

I kissed him with everything that I had in me.

I poured my fears, my love and my soul into the kiss that I placed on his lips.

I was sure.

I was ready.

He pulled away from me with a smile and then slowly pulled my knees apart.

He pushed me, lightly, so that I positioned myself on my back as he made himself comfortable between my thighs.

"Relax," he said.

I hadn't noticed that I was shaking until he spoke.

It wasn't that I was scared at this point. I was just excited, horny and ready for some action!

Shut up and put your damn mouth on it already!

And finally, Tristan did just that.

For the next hour or so, Tristan did things to me that I'd only seen on pornos or late night TV.

He did things to me that felt so good that I wanted to punch him in the top of the head or in the chest while he was doing them.

It was better than I'd ever imagined it would be.

It felt to me like crack felt to a crack head their very first time getting high.

Making love to him left me breathless.

Indeed losing my virginity to him had left me speechless and little did he know, he was going to need the stamina of three men for the next few days, because I had thirty years of making love, all the way to straight tearing it up, to make up for.

As Tristan wrapped his arms around me, I couldn't have felt more complete in my entire life.

It was the perfect ending, to a perfect night.

And this was only the beginning.

***

"Oh my, he popped that cherry didn't he?" My sister Cheyanne asked.

"He popped it all of a hundred times ago!" I laughed as she started to squeal and then proceeded to ask questions, begging for details.

Since that night, Tristan and I had been screwing like rabbits.

All over the house...and let's not mention the things that we'd done outside of the house or at the park, two restaurants...and did I mention the public library?

Don't judge me, but I just couldn't help myself.

Tristan was now talking wedding, and baby talk and the whole nine yards.

I was ecstatic at the thoughts of a future together. And the fact that I now had a steady *plus one.*

"I've never seen you like this before."

"That's because I've never been in love before...until now," I responded honestly.

Yes, I was absolutely in love with Tristan and I wasn't afraid to say it. I would shout it from the highest mountain if I could have.

I felt as though this, what we had, was the one thing that I'd always been missing.

I couldn't believe that I'd thought that I was happy without it and I would do anything that I could to make sure that I never had to live without it again.

Oh how I loved me some Tristan!

Cheyanne smiled at me and we continued to talk and enjoy our monthly outing that we made time to have with each other.

During our conversation, I saw that Delilah called twice back to back but I let her go to voicemail just like I always did.

I still hadn't spoken with her since she'd moved but her voicemails only said that she was just calling to see how I was doing.

In other words, she was just calling to be nosey, and I could do without her meddling.

Christmas was only two months away, so I figured that I would eventually need to call and speak to her, just to get the address to send a check for Bryson.

But that was about it.

My sister and I finished up our lunch and decided that we should definitely take the time to invite our other sister the next time that we got together.

Lauren was our other sister, but she damn sure didn't act like it.

Other than making sure that she sent her part to cover our mother's hospital expenses, we rarely heard from her.

She and her husband were both pediatricians, so of course their schedules were busy, but truth be told, that wasn't the only reason that she preferred to stay away.

And I knew why.

Before my sister Cheyanne married her husband, years ago, she had been engaged to an investment banker named Rodney.

I'd tried to tell her that I could see straight through Rodney's lying, cheating ass and I often told her that he was a wolf in sheep's clothing but Cheyanne was blind to his charm, his wit and his big bank account.

But all of the signs were there and I could see them as clear as day.

All she had to do was pay attention, but she didn't want to. Any, every, warning that you could think of was right there, front and center, but as I said, my sister didn't see it.

Oh maybe she did and just didn't want to admit it.

Anyway, long story short, I spotted him and our sister Lauren coming out of a hotel together one day.

Now, Lauren had always been odd, and an easy target for bullying and things of that nature coming up, but still, she knew right from wrong and no matter how invisible she may have felt, that didn't give her the right to sleep with her sister's fiancé a day before the wedding.

We were family and family didn't do that to one another.

Lauren was forever labeled as nasty as hell in my book and I was going to tell her just that that night at the rehearsal dinner.

I followed her outside only to find that she and Rodney were meeting to chat on the side of the restaurant.

I heard her tell him that she loved him and how Cheyanne always got the guy and how she felt that he should be with her and marrying her instead.

She told him that he was her *first* and that she just couldn't live without him.

She deserved to be smacked, but what he'd said to her, hurt her far more than me slapping her would have.

He told her that what she had meant nothing to him. He told her that it was fun but that he was still marrying Cheyanne. He even had the nerve to tell her that they could still have sex on the side even after he married our sister.

Nasty bastard!

Anyway, Lauren cried and said that that wasn't enough for her anymore and told him goodbye. She'd said that she couldn't stand to see them together and even said that she wouldn't be attending the wedding.

She ran off, crying, with her head in her hands.

Ever since that day, Lauren has kept her distance from us all.

Even though Cheyanne hadn't married him, she still never came around.

She'd even had a destination wedding to keep from being around us and didn't tell us that she'd had our niece until she was already a week old.

I wasn't sure if it was because she hated Cheyanne that much or if it was because he'd turned her down after he'd used her but whatever it was, it was enough to make her stay as far away from us as possible.

On the flip side, I told Cheyanne of my suspicious of Rodney and another woman that night once more, in one last attempt to save her from him and his *friendly* penis.

Though I had the proof, and solid facts, I couldn't bring myself to tell Cheyanne that it was her own sister that he was sleeping with so I lied and said that I'd overheard him on the phone with another woman.

Cheyanne still acted as though she didn't believe me and needed more proof but the next day right before saying I do, she looked at my face.

I told her with my eyes that I was telling the truth about him. I confirmed with the look on my face that I was indeed right about him and that she was making a huge mistake.

Simply reading and trusting the look on my face, she threw her flowers in his face and left him, mouth open, in shock at the altar.

I couldn't have been more proud of her at that very moment. She'd done the right thing.

The funny thing was that she hadn't put two and two together after Lauren dropped out of the wedding at the last minute saying that she was too sick to get out of bed to attend.

Cheyanne never even questioned her but Lord knows she should have.

But, anyway, that was years ago and it was far past time for us to do better with the whole sister bonding thing.

All three of us.

There was a time that we were as close as sisters could be and to be honest I missed those times. Though Lauren had always stayed to herself, her sisters were the only people that she'd let close to her.

Not to mention, that Cheyanne and I on several occasions had to go to war for her. We didn't play about Lauren. We didn't play about our blood.

But life was too short and even though Lauren acted as though she hated us, we all still loved her.

No one else really knew what her problem was. They simply used the excuse that she had always been odd, but I knew that it had something to do with the whole Cheyanne and Rodney situation, but I never told a soul.

I only hoped that one day she would get over it all, especially since now she was married, and simply come back around and be our sister like she used to be.

Maybe we could use our mother's birthday in the next few weeks to get her to come and hang with us.

Maybe.

After lunch, my sister and I parted ways and I called Tristan to see where he was.

"I'm at the bank. Where are you?"

"I was on my way home, but since you're not there, I'll go to the store. I'm going to get some candy for the trick-or-treaters tonight," I smiled as I spoke to him.

It was Halloween and though I wasn't particularly into the holiday, I just felt like giving.

"Oh, okay. By the way, would you mind if I brought a few extra things to your place? I'm there all the time anyway so I just figured---"

"Sure." I answered before he'd finished his sentence.

As long as I can spray it for roaches first!

Although I'd thought it, I dared not say it.

I didn't want to offend him, though I had been saying small things about picking up after himself a lot lately.

He didn't make much fuss about it.

He would simply do whatever it was that I'd said.

So, that showed that he was willing and I could work with the willing.

We got off of the phone and I headed to the store as planned.

Call me crazy, but it seemed that since I had been in a relationship, men had been coming from every direction; even more so than they always had.

It seemed like no matter where I went it was always someone trying to step to me.

I'd be lying if I said that I wasn't flattered.

I would also be lying if I said that I didn't size one or two of them up every now and then, because I did.

I'd seen a few that would have looked good by my side, a few others that seemed to be good *potentials*, but I had Tristan and he was more than enough for me.

Though there had been this one guy at the gas station that pumped my gas.

He'd asked me what my name was and immediately asked me to run away with him

He told me to quit my job and travel the word with him. Seeing that he was being chauffeured, I was sure that he had some *big boy* money.

He was attractive too.

But I had to decline.

He frowned when I told him that I was in a relationship and even said that I was still *fair game* since I wasn't married yet, but after seeing that I wasn't going anywhere, he kissed my hand and walked away.

Where had he been all of my life?

But luckily, the love that I had for Tristan was everything that I needed and he meant more to me than money.

He meant more to me than anything in the world.

And he assured me that he felt the same.

In the store, randomly I threw bags of candy into my cart.

I knew for a fact that Tristan had changed me. Never before had I even thought about passing out candy or doing something extra that I didn't have to do.

Never before had I been so happy and full of life, until Tristan came into my world.

I was always on cloud nine. I always felt so good.

Tristan had saved me in so many ways, and he would never understand just how truly thankful I was for him.

For some reason, after a while, I got the strangest feeling that someone was watching me.

I was right.

I turned around to see a woman that I didn't know, staring at me.

Being polite, I smiled at her but she didn't smile back.

Instead she acted as though she hadn't been looking at me at all.

But I wasn't stupid.

She had definitely been watching me.

I shrugged and concluded that maybe she liked my outfit or something and I continued picking up candy.

Once outside, I loaded the car with the bags and once I got in, like always, I started the car, placed on my sunglasses, even though it was October, glanced at myself in the mirror and then checked my surroundings.

And what do you know...

There she was---again!

She was sitting in her car, only a few spaces from me, just staring at me as if she wanted to punch me in the face.

The issue was that I didn't know her and I was sure that she didn't know me.

Judging by the car that she was in, sister had a few bucks I was sure, but that still didn't explain why she was watching me.

We made eye contact and this time she didn't even pretend as though she wasn't looking at me.

Instead she half smiled, or maybe it was a sarcastic smirk, whatever it was, she'd done it and then hastily drove away.

Who is she?

****

Chapter Five

My new assistant was working on my last nerve!

She was so damn slow!

And I'm not talking about just pace wise; oh no, she definitely had a few screws missing in that tiny little head of hers.

I'd wished that I'd seen this side of her during the interview process but I hadn't.

I felt as though I had been tricked, bamboozled.

Maybe she has a twin or something that interviewed for her because there was no way in hell that she the same nicely dressed, proper speaking woman that I'd interviewed that day.

And no one could tell me any different.

Nevertheless, I was trying to hang in there and give her a chance but she had better get her act together.

"Knock, knock," Hunter said knocking on my door.

I smiled at him and the tall, black gentleman that was with him.

I forced myself not to give him the full body exam.

I was already taken.

"Just wanted to introduce you to Karl. Karl this is Tori, our Senior Vice President. Karl is taking the management position that we had open since Lou took over for Richard," Hunter finished his introduction.

That job was supposed to have been Tristan's!

We'd watched for that phone call, but they'd never even called him for the interview.

Tristan asked everyday if anyone had said anything about the opening and I'd always asked him if he'd received a phone call.

He seemed to be losing faith and didn't understand why he hadn't gotten the call.

But now I know why.

If I had to guess, it was a personal hire for one of them. Either that or someone was owed a bigger favor than I was.

Either way, I was extremely disappointed for Tristan but I guess everything happens for some reason or another.

They disappeared and another knock came shortly after.

I looked up and it was Tristan.

He hadn't been back to my office since the day of the interview.

I smiled at him genuinely as I got an eyeful of his attire. He was always dressed to impress which was one thing that I loved about him.

I took pride in my appearance as well, so I loved that he did the same.

"And what have I done to deserve such a beautiful surprise?" I asked him, standing up to hug him.

My door was still open so I didn't want to do too much by giving him a kiss. I hadn't even told anyone at the office that I had a man yet.

"Well, I needed to see you," Tristan said rather timidly as he took a seat.

I could tell that something was wrong.

He was definitely acting out of character and his whole vibe was just off.

"What's wrong?" I asked him sincerely.

"I just got fired. Something about budget cutbacks," Tristan said.

"Really?" I asked him and reached for his hand.

Hearing the news not only made me feel bad for him, but it also made me a little angry.

The job here at our firm would have been perfect and right on time had they really considered him for the position like they were supposed to.

"Is there anything that I can do?"

Tristan just shook his head.

I wished that there was something that I could do. The idea of firing my assistant and giving him the job crossed my mind but I knew that now, he wouldn't take it.

Maybe before, but now that we were involved a position like that, under me, just wouldn't feel right to him.

"Well, everything is going to be okay. You'll have another job in no time. In the meantime, I got your back."

Did I just say that?

Geez, his love had definitely changed me!

***

It was the day before Thanksgiving, which was my mother's birthday.

Four of her five children were at the hospital.

Of course Lauren had called and sent gifts but hadn't shown up.

My mother seemed better, happier or maybe it was that she was just glad to be surrounded by all of us.

It felt good to see my brothers and sister, as well as their spouses and kids, all in one place.

Tristan was officially introduced to everyone and he appeared to have been having the time of his life as he chatted and shared conversations with my brothers and brother-in-law.

"So, will there be a wedding soon or what?" Cheyanne asked and my mother smiled in agreement.

I hoped so.

But I didn't think that it would be as soon as I'd hoped it would be.

Tristan was still looking for a new job and so far, he hadn't had much luck.

It hadn't been all that long yet but I could tell that he was becoming frustrated.

Of course my bank account was loaded and though I'd never been the type to want to help out a man in trouble with his finances, I was ready and willing to help Tristan if he needed me to.

But so far, he hadn't had to ask.

Hopefully some of the jobs would start reaching out to him soon but I was sure he had a good bit of savings to carry him for a while.

He was good with money, just as I was, so hopefully he always kept a stash for a rainy day.

"We will see," I finally responded to their question.

We talked about a few random things and then my mother decided to drop a bomb.

"I'm ready to come home."

My sister and I both looked at each other with surprise.

Personally, I couldn't believe my ears but it was about time.

She'd been ordered by a judge to be committed a few years ago for a certain amount of time but she had come and with all of the doctors suggestions and concerns and because she'd wanted to stay there, we'd just made sure that we paid the bill every month, even after she had served her time and was free to leave.

It was like one those crazy hospitals that you think of off the top of your head, no, it was the real expensive kind.

It was almost like an independent retirement community, except for crazy people.

We'd wanted to make sure that she was comfortable and for four thousand dollars a month, she'd definitely had better been.

But now she wanted to come home.

My situation had changed, but I was still willing to let her come and stay with me but instead she'd said that she wanted to be on her own.

We agreed to get everything situated for her and have her in a place as soon as possible.

It would be rather nice if she could finish living out her life the way that she was supposed to and without hiding in some hospital because she was scared to really face the reality of a broken heart.

But for some reason I got the feeling that she was back and that she was going to be just fine.

Who knows, maybe she would find love again.

Well, maybe that was pushing it a little.

Leaving the hospital, I felt so much joy in my heart.

I felt so much happiness.

As Tristan drove, I smiled and reached out for him to hold my hand.

He quickly glanced at it but instead of grabbing it, he peered back at the road as if he hadn't seen it.

What the hell was his problem?

I wanted to ask but decided that I wasn't in the mood for an argument, so I turned to look out the window instead.

We hadn't argued too many times, but when we had, they lasted for hours.

He wouldn't stop until he got his point across, and I wouldn't stop until I had the last word, because nine times out of ten, I was right.

But as I said, we'd only had a few disagreements.

Once we arrived home, I gave him all the signs that I wanted to be a little naughty but he ignored them.

I couldn't have been any clearer if I'd stripped down butt naked and bent over, but he didn't seem to be paying me any attention.

I was confused by his actions.

While visiting my mother, he seemed just fine so what was his problem all of a sudden?

"Tristan, what's wrong?"

At first he didn't say anything but once I stood in front of the television, he finally looked at me and spoke.

"You told your brothers' that I lost my job."

In all honesty, I had only mentioned it to the oldest one to see if he knew of anyone that was hiring.

"I'm sorry. I was just trying to help."

"How? By making me look bad?"

His tone was different and I didn't like the hostility in his voice so I tried to defuse the situation.

"I'm sorry."

"Yeah, I know."

Tristan sat back on the couch and picked up the remote.

I guess maybe I had overstepped a boundary or two but I was just trying to help. He'd been so stressed since he'd lost his job and I was just trying to get him back on the right track.

But he was a man and I guess I had to let him be one and find his own way.

So, I guess I had some making up to do.

I inched closer to him.

"Move Tori."

I ignored his request and got down on my knees right in front of him.

I reached for his zipper and he swatted at my hand for all of two seconds before he allowed me to tug on the zipper and unbutton his pants.

I smiled at how easy he was to become submissive.

And with that thought, I freed his protruding penis and I *apologized*...with my throat of course.

***

I smiled as the delivery man sat the roses on my desk.

Someone must be in a good mood today, I thought as I reached for my phone to call Tristan.

To my surprise, he didn't pick up so I called again, but still I didn't get any answer.

It was the middle of the day and since he still didn't have a job, I wondered what it was that he was doing.

The holidays had come and gone and it was now March and Tristan still hadn't found work.

I had put in at least a hundred applications for him online, but we hadn't had any luck as of yet.

But I was glad that he wasn't as down and out as he had been in the beginning.

As far as I knew, he was simply using what money he did have wisely, and continuing to look for work.

I'd questioned him about filing for unemployment but he refused initially and so I could only assume that whatever was in his bank account was enough to carry him for a while.

I found it sweet that even though he had to be cautious with his spending, he still decided to do something to make my day.

If only he had answered his phone so that I could have told him Thank You.

My phone started to vibrate and I hurriedly picked it up assuming that it was Tristan but it wasn't, it was Delilah.

I'd only spoken to her briefly around Christmas time to check on Bryson and send her some money as my Christmas gift to him.

I was very short with her and limited with my words when we'd spoken. I'd stayed on the phone with her for all of five minutes but she still didn't seem to be getting the hint.

Against my better judgment, I answered the phone.

"Hi! I'm surprised that you answered. You're kind of hard to reach these days," Delilah said.

I didn't respond to her comment so she continued.

"Well, I need to talk to you about something," she said.

I immediately rolled my eyes.

I could only imagine what it was and to be honest, unless it had to do with Bryson, I really didn't care.

But just as Delilah started her next sentence, Tristan beeped in on my other line.

"Delilah, I'll call you back as soon as I get some free time and we can talk then," I said to her, clicking over to the other line before she'd even had a chance to respond.

"Hey baby, thanks for the flowers," I said.

"What flowers?" Tristan questioned.

"The roses that you had delivered to me just a little while ago silly," I said to him.

"I didn't send any roses Tori," Tristan said and by the sound of his voice I could tell that he was serious.

I got up to look at the flowers and to search for a note or a card. There wasn't one.

Well who else would send me flowers?

"Who are they from?"

"I don't know. There isn't a card. I thought they were from you," I answered him honestly.

Surprisingly he didn't continue to question me about them, which told me that he had been the one to send them and was lying or playing some kind of trick.

Knowing the way that he was, he would have continued asking about them and dying to know where they had come from, so I smelled them and rolled my eyes, deciding to play along with his little joke.

Saying nothing else about the flowers, Tristan began to talk about starting his own business, which definitely had my interest.

I was all ears when it came to following your dreams and taking that step toward entrepreneurship.

But then things went in a different direction.

I'd assumed that he was talking about starting his own accounting firm and maybe even trying to take some of the loyal customers that he had dealt with for years with him but instead he said something about opening a chain of laundromats.

I can't really say that it was a terrible idea.

It wasn't.

It was actually an okay idea if he had them built in uptown areas or close to colleges or maybe even in low income areas.

Someone was always bound to need a laundromat. But like I said, it was in a totally different direction.

Tristan was so professional and I just thought that he wanted to stay in that line of work.

But obviously, he was on to his next dream.

I guess it wasn't all that bad.

We talked for a few minutes more, than I had to let him go to prepare for a meeting.

I thought more about his business venture and figured that it could actually bring in a good amount of cash.

Tristan stated that I could join in as a partner if I'd like to, and I might just have to take him up on his offer.

After all, I did have plenty of extra funds to take a few risks with and we were both good with money and numbers so maybe we could make this thing happen.

Together.

Yes, I liked the sound of that.

***

"Well, where are you now?"

"I came by my house for a second. I'll be there in a few."

Though Tristan had been staying over at my place for a while now, of course he still had his own house.

It was paid for and his, so at the end of the day, we could always fix it up and sale it if we needed to.

I couldn't help but wonder what he was doing over there. I surely hoped that he wasn't planning on bringing more junk to pile up at my house.

There wasn't any more room for anymore clutter.

Living with him, more or less, had definitely taken some getting used to.

We were completely different when it came to keeping house and respecting each other's personal belongings and some days I wanted to go through the whole house and label "Do not Touch!" on all of my stuff.

I grew up with four other siblings and although there were plenty of times that space was limited, we learned to keep our hands off of what didn't belong to us and to respect each other's property.

Tristan didn't know a thing about that.

The other day I walked in on him using my deodorant.

Maybe that isn't a big issue for some but for me...I damn near had a fit!

Have you seen the amount of hair that men keep under their arms?

Go get your own damn deodorant!

I'm just saying.

And then he didn't even bother to go out and get him some, even though he knew that he was out.

So, I suggested a late night *Walmart* run.

I know it seems petty, but that was only one of the many things that drove me crazy.

I'd never lived with a man before so I didn't know what to expect, but secretly I prayed every night that he would wake up the next day and decide to go back home.

Oh, but I still loved him though.

He had been working day and night, brainstorming and coming up with ideas for the laundromats.

I was glad to see that he was at least trying to be productive instead of sitting by the phone all day waiting for it to ring.

Speaking of, I'd found the time to ask Hunter, my boss, about clearly passing over Tristan for the position but to my surprise he stated that they contacted him at least ten times before even pursuing other candidates.

I found that unbelievable, especially since Tristan wanted that job with everything in him.

He'd been waiting for that phone call like the old folks were waiting for the Rapture; watching day and night.

Ready.

And I know for a fact that they had the correct number because I'd emailed it to Hunter that same day.

Something just wasn't adding up.

I was sure that Hunter didn't have anything to do with the mix-up but I couldn't say the same about the rest of them.

I was sure that a few of them didn't like me all that much, until they needed me to do something for them. But I could have cared less whether they liked me or not.

No one was going to mess up my check.

It was just that simple.

With Tristan still out, I decided to do a full house cleaning.

And little did he know whatever I found on the floor was going in the damn trash!

And I ain't playing!

After two hours of cleaning, and scrubbing and sweeping and moping, I realized that Tristan still hadn't made it in.

I found my phone, which I'd accidently thrown in the trash, and gave him a call.

He didn't answer.

Here lately, that had started to become the normal.

And my mind was definitely starting to wonder.

I was different when it came to certain things and a lot different and less judgmental than I used to be. But don't give me a door or an opening, unless you wanted me to step through it.

Because trust me, I would.

Why wasn't he answering his phone?

Before I had a chance to talk myself out of it, I grabbed my keys and my purse and headed out the door.

Maybe I was overreacting or maybe I wasn't, but we were about to find out.

I pulled up at Tristan's house and to my surprise, his car wasn't there...but another car was.

Without hesitation, I got out of my car and headed to the front door.

Instead of knocking, I tried to use my key except...it didn't work.

What the hell is going on here?

Just as I balled up my hand to knock, the front door flew open.

"Can I help you?" she asked.

Oh, you have got to be kidding me!

I looked at the woman standing in front of me.

She was pretty, I guess if you liked the whole light-skinned, hazel eyed chicks, but she still didn't have a thing on me.

But at the end of the day, she could have been the ugliest woman I'd ever seen and it wouldn't have made a damn difference.

Tristan was a dead man!

I was so furious that I was beginning to see red.

You mean to tell me that all of this time a woman had been staying at his house?

A woman was staying at Tristan's house?

I glanced down at her hand.

And not only was she wearing a ring...but also a band.

Wait a damn minute...so he's married?

Though she was innocent in the matter, I felt as though I wanted to push her down.

I know, after all, she was the wife apparently, so I had no right but that's how I felt.

How did I miss that?

How didn't I see this?

How did I miss the signs?

Come to think of it, there were none.

At least not any that pointed towards a wife.

"Who are you?"

I was just going to walk away but instead, I decided that she deserved to know the truth.

"I'm Tori. Where is Tristan?"

"Who?"

What did she mean *who*?

"Tristan? He lives here. Well, at least he owns this house."

"I'm sorry you must have the wrong house. Me and my husband, George, owns this house," she said, nodding to the truck that was pulling up on the other side of my car.

George was a white man.

I let out a deep breath.

Though things still weren't adding up, at least she wasn't his wife.

She went on to tell me that the house had been seized by the bank and that her and her husband had gotten an incredible deal on it.

After I apologized for bothering her I hurried to my car and got in.

Tristan was a s good as dead!

One thing I did not tolerate was lies or secrets and boy did he have some explaining to do!

I was sure that I had been at the right house.

I'd been there with him several times, so I knew that that was the house and that he at least used to live there.

Why didn't he tell me that the bank had taken it?

Had they taken it because he lost his job?

I thought he told me that it was paid for.

But what I was even more upset about was the fact that he'd just told me that he was at the house.

At what house?

You don't have a damn house!

I was livid but one thing was for sure, Tristan had better have one hell of a reason for his actions or...

I don't even have to say it!

****

Chapter Six

"Is there anything else you want me to do?" Tristan asked.

I simply shook my head and he exited the room.

Where do I begin?

So, for starters, I found out the hard way that Tristan was a liar, which now had me questioning everything that he said.

After showing up at his so-called house that day, only to find out that it wasn't his house at all anymore, I headed home to wait for him.

"Where you been?" I'd asked him.

"I told you I was at my house. I was looking for a few things."

As soon as he'd finished his sentence, I threw my shoe at him.

I told him that I knew the truth and that I'd went by his so-called house and that he wasn't there...better yet, it was no longer his house at all.

Real quick, his house was then described as...his storage.

Tristan told me that the bank took the house a little after he lost his job.

He said that he'd taken out a second mortgage on it when dealing with his father and his medical bills. He'd explained that he'd tried to keep it but in order to keep it, it would have taken everything that he had in his savings and then some.

He'd said he couldn't bring himself to ask me for help so he had no choice. He said that he didn't know how to tell me because he didn't want me to think any less of him.

Pretty much, he had a decent excuse, and had the paperwork from the bank to prove it.

But still yet, that was no reason to lie.

You don't lie under any circumstances, not to people that you say that you love.

Did I forgive him?

Unfortunately I did.

For two reasons.

One, I could see how the male ego could come into play. He was already feeling down about losing his job and then on top of that he lost his house.

I get it.

He was ashamed and embarrassed. Though lying was definitely the wrong way to go about it, I still somewhat understood.

And number two, well, did I mention that I was six weeks pregnant?

Yep, I was expecting.

I'd found out only two days after the whole situation and the lie about the house came out.

I was so frustrated and undecided about what I was going to do and what was next for us.

The whole thing really had me stressed out.

Any other time he would have been dismissed with the quickness, but I was on the fence.

He had definitely made me *soft.* For some reason I couldn't just drop him like I normally do men and keep it moving.

Hell, where was he going to go?

He didn't have a house anymore.

But lying was one thing that I just couldn't stand and it bothered me that I couldn't come up with a solution as fast as I'd wanted to.

Nevertheless, I wasn't eating or sleeping and that Monday morning, as I headed for my office, I passed out.

Next thing I know, I was waking up in a hospital room with Tristan and my sister Cheyanne by my side.

And that's when I was hit with the big news.

I was pregnant.

Let me explain something to you, this isn't exactly all going according to my plan.

I didn't expect to be having a baby before I was married. But I guess that's always been my problem.

I thought that I could plan my entire life instead of just going with the flow.

And it was past time for me to start just going with life and figuring it out along the way.

So with the news, Tristan's lie seemed so small and I wiped his slate clean with the threat that it was definitely a onetime thing and there would be no second, third or fourth time.

He agreed and vowed not to let his ego get in our way again.

For now, only Tristan, Cheyanne and myself, knew about the baby.

I was going to announce it to my mother and the rest of my siblings when the time was right.

It had only been a week since we'd found out and I'd been instructed to take two or three days off from work but seven sounded so much better.

It was now Sunday, and I was lying in bed with my feet up, resting while Tristan ran around the house doing everything that I asked him to do.

He was still on punishment from the *na-na*, but other than that, I hadn't been as mean to him as I could have been.

He was forgiven and I was trying to let it go.

I couldn't help but lay there and think about the baby.

I'd thought about kids before, but I guess in a way, I didn't think that I would ever really get to have them.

It seemed as though I was getting everything that I had been lacking and I could only conclude that everything was happening according to plan.

Somewhere, somehow, I must've fallen asleep because the next time I opened my eyes, the room was pitch black.

"Tristan!"

I waited to hear the sound of his footsteps coming down the hall, but I heard nothing.

I could hear him chattering so I called his name again but he still didn't come.

Rolling my eyes, I got out of bed and headed up the hall but when I got into the living room, Tristan's face was buried in the couch and he appeared to be sleeping.

Huh?

I know damn well that I'd just heard him talking.

He didn't turn around and he was even slightly snoring.

Maybe I was imagining things, I thought, and I decided that I was going to head to the kitchen for a snack, but just as I turned to walk away I heard a low voice.

"Hello? Hello?"

I turned around in a hurry and smacked the back of Tristan's head.

"Give me the damn phone," I said and held out my hand.

He looked at me as if he had really been asleep.

Really?

His phone was in his hand and though the screen wasn't lit up, the voice was still saying the word *hello*.

"Give me the phone or pack your stuff and get out," I said to him in a tone that told him that I was dead ass serious.

He darn near threw the phone in my direction.

I guess maybe threatening to put him out on the street was kind of harsh, but oh well.

"Hello? Who is this?"

"Tori? How---where---where is Tristan?" my sister Cheyanne asked.

"Cheyanne? What are you doing talking to Tristan at this time of night? What were y'all talking about?" I quizzed her.

"Why?" she said.

I blacked out for all of two seconds.

I shook my head and tried to get myself together.

Why?

What the hell did she mean why?

"Um, I would think that I have the right to know why you are talking to my man," I stated in frustration.

"Maybe. But not when what we were discussing pertains to me and my relationship. I needed his advice. I got it. Tell him I said thank you. Bye."

And with that, she hung up in my face.

My mouth was hanging wide open.

I didn't know whether to call her back and curse her out or to get in my car and drive all the way to her house just to smack the crap out of her.

"What was that about?" I asked him, throwing his phone on the table and placing my hand on my hip.

"What did she say?"

What?

Is he serious?

"It doesn't matter what she said. Why is my sister calling you late at night Tristan?"

"She needed some advice."

Well, at least their answers were the same.

"Well, if it was all innocent, why try to pretend to be asleep and act as though you weren't on the phone?"

Tristan sat there for a second.

"Because you're mean lately, and I didn't want to hear you fuss. Maybe it's because you're pregnant but I just wanted to avoid hearing your mouth."

Maybe it's because I'm pregnant?

No stupid, it's because you're a liar!

Well, or at least because he told a lie.

He knew darn well that the pregnancy wasn't my reason for being a little snappy at him lately but hearing him actually voice that I was *mean*, sort of made me feel bad.

At the end of the day, I didn't want to push him away. Especially not now with me being pregnant and all.

Of course being a single mother left a bad taste in my mouth and other than that I still loved him to death.

Maybe I was acting just a little bit mean, but it was his fault.

Still, I didn't like the whole sneaking and talking to my sister thing, and then when questioned, they both acted as though what they were talking about was none of my business.

I didn't like that at all.

I didn't even know that they had each other's phone numbers, but for now, I was going to let it go.

But best believe it was only for now.

"Come on and drive me to somebody's drive-thru. We're hungry." I said to Tristan and he got up to get himself together.

The next morning came all too soon.

I definitely didn't want to go back to work but I knew that I had to.

Hell, both of us couldn't be unemployed.

I hadn't heard Tristan mention much about the laundromat idea lately, maybe that was because in his words, I had been being mean, but with a baby on the way, he surely had to make a move and he had better do it fast!

I very well had the financial means to take care of the baby by myself, but I wasn't going to.

Nope, I just wasn't going to do it.

He was going to do his part and I was going to make sure of it.

I forced myself out of bed and within the next hour I was out the door and headed to the money.

I made sure that I made as much noise as possible to wake Tristan.

If I couldn't sleep in, neither could he.

I'd decided not to inform the office of my pregnancy just yet.

I was still trying to get use to the idea, so I figured that I wouldn't break the news to them until I was showing and could no longer hide it.

After parking my car, like every work morning, I walked across the street to get an expresso.

I'd heard that I was going to have to stop drinking them while pregnant, but that was going to take some time.

My day just didn't go right unless I had at least one.

Even on weekends, I came all the way across town, to this very spot, just to get one.

The line was longer than usual but I didn't mind being a few minutes late.

On these mornings, I did somewhat miss Delilah.

She would always wait until I arrived to work, to walk over with me.

Thinking of her, I never did give her a call back so that she could tell me whatever it was that she needed to tell me.

Maybe I would do that, sooner or later.

After finally making it to the front of the line, I smiled once I was finally able to feel the cup in my hands.

I paid for my expresso and turned around...

"Ahh!"

I screamed as the entire, hot expresso spilled all over my chest.

The people around me immediately tried to help me by grabbing napkins and some even tried to wipe it from my chest even though it was extremely inappropriate.

"I'm sorry. I didn't mean to bump into you. I didn't see you," she said.

By the time I followed the voice and looked in her direction, she was heading out the door.

She glanced back once she was outside, just before she crossed the street.

It was her!

That b---

"Ma'am? Are you okay? Here, we got you another expresso on the house and a gift card," the young gentleman said from behind the counter but my focus was still trying to see which way the *stalker lady* had gone, but she was out of sight.

It was the same woman that had been staring at me at the store way back on Halloween.

It was obvious that she had followed me there, which made me wonder if she had been watching me the entire time.

Did she know where I live?

Obviously she knew where I worked.

I'd never seen her a day in my life before the time at the store so I was sure that whatever the reason it was that she was following me had nothing to do with me.

But I was sure it had something to do with somebody.

Tristan.

With a wet blouse, I walked out of the coffee shop, with my new expresso and my gift card and headed to the office.

I was the a top executive, so of course I had a bathroom in my office where I could clean up and I always kept a change of clothes there just in case of some type of emergency.

Everyone stared as I made my way to my office and shut the door behind me.

I couldn't help but smile at the office full of balloons, cards and flowers.

Everyone must've heard about me fainting the week before.

Another set of red roses, in the same type of vase was sitting on my desk.

They still didn't have a card but I was sure that they were from Tristan.

I headed to the bathroom to get myself together.

Today just wasn't a good day...

"Just ride with me, please."

"Tristan, I don't feel like it. You wouldn't believe the day that I've had. My expresso spilled all over my shirt this morning. I think I lost a client. And I didn't do half of the work that I was supposed to do. I just want to go to sleep and start all over again tomorrow."

I didn't want to tell him about the strange woman just yet. I had a little investigating of my own to do first.

"Please."

I looked at him and finally nodded my head yes.

As soon as we got into the car and he started to drive, I dozed off.

I dreamt of my childhood.

I thought of how everyone wanted to be us...except us.

They assumed we had the perfect life.

My parents appeared to have been the perfect couple.

We were in the church. We had a fairly nice house and car back in those days.

Everybody thought that life for us was good.

But they didn't see the never ending bible studies or the scripture quizzes that took place instead of allowing us to go out and enjoy a nice spring day or the warmth of the summer sun.

We never really got the chance just to be kids.

We all acted as though our childhood hadn't affected us but it had.

It molded us into who we were today.

So, in a way, I guess it hadn't been a bad thing.

The next time I opened my eyes, we were at a vineyard.

It was one that I'd always passed but never seemed to have the time to stop.

It was around six o'clock in the evening and starting to get dark.

It was April, but surprisingly it was clear and not as many showers as we usually saw around this time of year.

Tristan got out of the car and opened my door.

Feeling as tired as ever, I got out of the car and Tristan grabbed my hand.

We walked through the entrance way and after turning the corner of the stone wall, I gasped in disbelief.

My family smiled at the sight of me and I smiled back.

Everyone was there, except my father of course, but I was used to him not being in attendance.

Even my sister Lauren and her family were there.

"What is this?"

"Well, your birthday is coming up and this is your birthday present," Tristan said.

I looked around at all of the decorations.

It was all decorated in lavender and ivory.

There were tall vases of lilies, surrounded by candlelight. There was a miniature waterfall, and diamonds and crystals and so much more.

It was very elegant.

A little *too* elegant.

I looked back at Tristan who was looking at my mother.

I'd just noticed how she was dressed and that she was holding a bible.

I looked back at Tristan confused.

He just smiled and then...

Everyone squealed as he got down on one knee.

Was he serious?

Was this was really happening?

But how?

Why?

Tristan went into his pocket and pulled out a beautiful, gorgeous, out of a magazine diamond ring.

Where in the hell did he get the money to pay for that?

Tori get it together. The man is trying to propose.

I chastised myself and then paid attention to the matter at hand.

"Marry me. Right here. Right now. I love you and I want to spend the rest of my life with you. It's only been about a year but it has been the best year of my life. Say you'll be my wife. Hopefully your mother didn't get ordained for nothing," Tristan joked.

I glanced at my mother.

I couldn't believe that she'd gotten ordained just to be able to marry me.

How sweet was that?

Oh, I felt so special!

But marriage?

This isn't exactly the way I imagined it.

It wasn't the hundred thousand dollar wedding that I'd always dreamed about.

Where was my white wedding gown and my oversized wedding party?

Where was the singing and the hundreds of people in attendance?

But maybe this wasn't so bad.

Maybe this was all that I need.

My family was here and that was all that really mattered.

I could always do the wedding of my dreams at a later time, right?

Was I really considering getting married?

And was Tristan the right man to be getting married to?

Before recently, my answer would have been heck yeah, but now...

Um....

Well...

You know what....

Screw it!

I'm taking this chance and if it doesn't work out---

"Yes!"

"Yes?"

"Yes."

Everyone cheered and Tristan placed the ring on my finger.

Everyone moved around as if they were waiting for my response.

Out of nowhere, a piano started playing and this show was on the road.

It all happened so fast and it was over in a flash.

It wasn't until we'd kissed that it really, really sunk in.

I was married now!

Wow, I couldn't believe it!

"Congratulations!" My sister Cheyanne squealed as she hugged me.

"I'm sorry for last night but we were getting the last few details together and we wanted it to be a surprise. I had to come up with something. I'm sorry if I was rude," she said apologetic and kissed my cheek.

I forgave her instantly and hugged her as tight as I could.

Who knew that they'd had something as wonderful as this up their sleeves!

"Well, how do you feel?" Mama asked me as she hugged me and kissed my cheek.

"I feel great! I'm so glad that you were here to share this day with me," I said to her sincerely.

"We'd tried to get your father here. I'd found him and left him a message on his voicemail hoping that he would've been here to walk you down the aisle, but he didn't show. I wanted this day to be perfect. Sorry," Tristan said, joining in on the conversation.

I smiled at him.

He definitely deserved an A for all of his effort.

Was I disappointed that my father hadn't showed up?

Nope, not at all.

He hadn't been at any of the others weddings either. Nor had he ever been around for any major occasions or events.

We'd all learned to accept that a long time ago.

"Today was perfect," I said to my husband.

I had a husband!

And I couldn't believe it!

***

I requested another two weeks off from work the day after the wedding.

I hadn't told Hunter my big news yet, only that I wasn't feeling well and that I needed to cash in on a few more sick days.

Though he wasn't the happiest about it, he agreed to more time off stating that I'd given them more than enough of my time and that overworking may have been the cause of me passing out and not feeling well.

So with the agreement that I'd check my emails, and tend to urgent matters, I was now free to spend the next two weeks with my brand new husband.

After a brief nap, I woke up to the smell of bacon.

It was half past noon, but breakfast was good for me anytime of the day.

"Good afternoon Mrs. Hall," Tristan smiled.

The word *Mrs* was like music to my ears!

I still couldn't believe that I'd actually gone through with it, but what was life if you didn't take chances?

I'd played the game, safely, for way too long.

And after almost thirty years of life, I was finally about to start enjoying the simple things.

The things that I'd always wanted, but always pretended that it was okay not to have them.

I was newly pregnant and newly married.

Life was good.

After eating, our breakfast for *lunch*, I didn't hesitate to bring up the conversation about employment.

The *old* me would have never married a man in this situation, but I was trying to see past the surface and there was no denying that I was head over heels in love with him.

But this brother needed a steady paycheck or something.

Point. Blank. Period.

"So, have you thought anything more about the laundromat idea? Or are you just going to go back to work?"

Tristan took some time to answer me.

As though he was thinking about which direction would be the better road to travel with a new baby and new wife and all.

"Well, I'd looked at some numbers and properties. And I've found two locations already. It's just---,"

"Just what?"

"I don't have enough in my savings to cover it all," Tristan finally let me in a little concerning his funds.

But this was only the beginning.

We were husband and wife now so money was a discussion that we needed to have.

Well, his money was a discussion that we needed to have.

He didn't need to know anything about mine.

"Well, how much?"

He looked at me as if I was speaking a foreign language.

I figured that I may as well invest in his dream since it was going to be a part of my future and with me on his team, there was nothing that he couldn't accomplish.

"$60,000," he stated timidly.

I got up from the chair and headed to my purse.

I wrote him a check for the amount and turned to face him.

"As long as I'm a partner in this and I want half the rights to the business and everything. Do we have a deal?"

Tristan smiled and stood to his feet.

He kissed me before taking the check from my hand.

"Deal."

So let's get this show on the road!

****

Chapter Seven

Tristan's snoring was making it impossible for me to sleep, so I got out of bed and headed for the living room to watch a little TV.

I glanced briefly at his paperwork on the coffee table and then I noticed that his phone was sitting beside it.

Don't do it Tori.

Here lately, I'd been trying my best not go looking for trouble.

I had been trying to change my ways and the way that I thought about things.

I didn't want to live my life always looking for the worst, and waiting for the right sign to end a relationship.

I just wanted to be happy and I was tired of letting my ways get in the way of that.

But...

To hell with that nonsense!

I picked up his phone.

Surprisingly, there was *now* a lock on it.

I wondered when he'd decided that he needed a little *extra* privacy.

I tried to guess the pin number to the lock, but my attempt failed.

What could it be?

At this point, I knew that maybe I should have just placed the phone back down, and just leave well enough alone.

All I had to do was mind my business and everything would be okay.

I'd always heard that a nosey person always seemed to get their feelings hurt.

Hell I'd even known this to be true first hand.

There was a time, years ago, when I'd dated a guy that I thought could have been someone special.

Our relationship was fresh, but it had started off with a bang and I was interested in seeing where we would end up.

Except one night, much like tonight, I decided to take a peek in his phone while he was passed out, counting sheep.

Boy did I regret that decision.

I'd never seen so many big, black *cocks* in one place, at one time, in my entire life!

And half of the photos had him in them…with the penises in places that I'd rather not force myself to remember.

I was his *cover up* or at least he was attempting to make me as such, because he was as down low, in the closet, as they came.

But I wouldn't have known that…if I hadn't gone through his phone.

So, with that in mind, snooping was no longer a bad thing.

It was a blessing.

I guessed Tristan's pin again but it was wrong, so I put my thinking cap on.

He was in Accounting, so his thinking strategy with things like this had to be similar to mine.

We were very good with numbers, but secretly, we would have loved it if it was as simple as 1-2-3.

That's it.

I typed in 1-2-3-4 and what do you know…it was correct!

I didn't know where to begin, so I headed to the texts messages.

There wasn't a single message there, not even from me.

The old me would have saw it as a *small* sign.

Why is he erasing his messages?

But the new me attempted to see it as no big deal.

The only calls in his call log were from that day, and the day before which was a total of five.

All from me and two outgoing to 1800 numbers.

I'd been around him and heard his phone ring several times, just that day, so I knew that there should have been way more than five calls in his call history; which meant, that Tristan had erased those too.

I was definitely starting to feel some kind of way on the inside.

Something just wasn't right.

I headed to check his pictures, but of course there was nothing there to see.

Tori, you are overreacting.

Maybe I was thinking too much about it and making it something that it wasn't.

I guess I was just looking for something that wasn't there.

I took a deep breath and dropped the phone on top of the stack of papers.

I headed to the kitchen for a snack.

When I returned, the phone was lit so of course, I looked to see what was going on with it.

It was an email notification at the top of the phone.

I hadn't bothered to check his email.

Looking at the new email, it seemed to be something that could have been marked as spam.

I did him a favor by going ahead and deleting the email but I didn't stop there.

Cautiously, I continued to scroll down the list of emails that had already been read.

For a while, I saw nothing and then I saw something that caught my eye.

It was from *my* job.

It was an email from the Accounting firm and from Richard's old assistant.

The email said:

Tristan,

We've contacted you numerous of times for an interview for an open position. You come highly recommended by one of our top executives, and we would love the opportunity to sit down with you and see if the current opening is a good fit for you. We've contacted you via phone but have been unsuccessful with reaching you. If we do not hear back from you, soon, we will assume that you are no longer interested in working for our company and will pursue other candidates. Please get back to us as soon as possible. Thank you.

I couldn't believe my eyes.

The email had come weeks ago and it showed that he'd read it, but hadn't bothered to respond to it.

So, if he got the email that also meant that he more than likely received the phone calls too.

Something just didn't make sense.

I was so confused.

Why had he lied?

Why hadn't he taken the calls or responded to the email?

He'd wanted that job so badly, so I just didn't understand what was going on with him or why he'd basically rejected the opportunity.

I wasn't sure what was going on with him or what the truth was behind his actions, but I was surely going to find out.

I exited out of his email and placed the phone in the exact place that I'd found it.

I sat the potato chips down on the coffee table as well.

I no longer had an appetite.

I simply sat in silence for the next hour or so, trying to get my thoughts together.

Just to be clear, the new Tori, happy about life, eager to take chances...was dead.

She had been hit by an invisible bus, carried to the morgue and currently awaiting to be thrown under six feet of dirt.

But now the *old* Tori, the one that was fierce, strong-willed, and always on top of everything and everybody...was back!

It was time to get my head back into the game and start paying more attention.

And if I had to guess, I would say that only a few days ago, I'd made one of the biggest mistakes of my life.

Damn.

***

"You have a fever of 104. I'm taking you to the hospital Tori."

"No, I'm not going to the hospital. I'll be fine," I'd been declining to go to the hospital for the last few hours and I was starting to sound like a broken record.

Tristan continued to dress me as though I hadn't said a word.

I swatted him away but he diligently continued to put my clothes on.

I'd woken up the next morning feeling terrible.

At first, I thought that my mind and my body were simply in a slump as a result of the bull crap that I'd seen the night before but when I got a fever, I knew that that wasn't it.

And once the fever came, things just seemed to get worse from there.

I was throwing up all over the place and I was becoming more and more concerned about my unborn child.

I couldn't keep anything down, not even water, so finally I stopped fighting Tristan, and let him take me to the hospital.

After hours of testing, I was committed for a rare case of meningitis.

The doctors said that if I hadn't gotten there when I had, there's no for sure way of saying what would have happened to me or the baby.

Basically, I would have died.

Tristan had saved my life and our child's life.

And for that, I was forever thankful.

I was in and out for the rest of the evening but every time that I opened my eyes, Tristan was right there by my side.

He held my hand, he prayed for my healing.

His actions not only surprised me but touched the deepest part of my heart.

I had never heard him pray before, and it shocked me that he knew how. The fact that he'd thought to pray over me, made me feel all tingly inside.

It impressed me.

No, I hadn't forgotten about the job incident and I was still going to bring it up when I was feeling better, but it was things such as this that made me fall in love with him all over again.

It made me *second-guess* myself and bringing up something like that, right now, wasn't the time.

In a way, the failure to respond to the calls and email didn't really even matter since he was starting the laundromats.

So, if he was no longer interested in the job, that's all that he had to say.

But instead, he'd said nothing. He'd just pretended as though he hadn't heard a thing about the position.

And with that being said, lies deserved to be confronted.

And it was my duty to mention my concerns to him when I was feeling better.

The next day, surprisingly, they allowed me to go home.

I wanted to stay a while longer, just to make sure that the baby and I were going to be okay, but they assured me that I was going to survive.

Once home, Tristan catered to my every need.

He even gave me a little bell to ring so that I didn't have to lift a finger.

I'd asked him to bring me a glass of orange juice and he informed me that we were all out.

He'd left, saying that he was going to the store and that he would be right back.

My phone immediately began to ring once I heard the front door close, and I assumed that it was him but it wasn't.

It was Delilah.

I was still ignoring her for the most part, but she was still calling.

I concluded that either she was just stupid for not seeing that I didn't want to talk to her or either she just didn't care.

But even though I wasn't feeling well, I remembered that she'd said that she had something to tell me, so I answered instead of sending her to voicemail.

"Hi, how are you?"

"I'm sick. How are you and Bryson?" I asked her.

She stated that they were doing well and then she got straight to the point.

"I was wondering if you ever found a new assistant?" Delilah asked.

"Of course I did."

"Oh, because, we are moving back so I was just wondering," she said.

She was moving back...why?

"I thought you were going to stay there with your folks?"

"I was but things aren't working out so, I was planning to come back. I wanted to ask you if Bryson and I could stay with you until we found a place."

Hell no!

I didn't say it out loud but I wanted to.

Not only did I not like her enough to allow her to live in my house, I now had a husband and no other woman was going to be in my house, around my man.

That was a disaster waiting to happen.

"Delilah, I got married, so living with me isn't going to work for me."

"What? You got married? When? To who?"

"His name is Tristan..."

"What did you say?"

"I said, his name is Tristan---Hall. Why do you know him?"

Delilah's silence made me uncomfortable.

After a while, she finally spoke.

"You damn right I know him. He's Bryson's *real* father."

***

I was waiting for Delilah and Bryson to land.

I was hoping that she had the wrong Tristan Hall but we were about to find out.

The day before yesterday, Delilah explained to me that Bryson's father wasn't who I thought it was.

She'd been lying the whole time.

She'd said that the man that she initially blamed it on eventually asked for a blood test and when the results stated that baby Bryson wasn't his, she'd known that it could only be one other man's.

Delilah said that she'd contacted *Tristan* and he agreed to a paternity test.

He was Bryson's father.

Well, more like his sperm donor because she'd said that even after finding out that he was his son, he hadn't done a thing for him and had only seen him once.

She said he just basically disappeared.

Delilah said she didn't feel the need to tell me that she'd found the real father of her child simply because I was the one that helped her with him and she didn't want anything to change.

What was even more shocking, she told me that the sex hadn't been consensual.

She said that Tristan had raped her.

Delilah said she'd met him years ago. She invited him over for conversation and a movie, but things went left.

I knew right then and there that she couldn't have been talking about my husband Tristan.

Tristan was so patient and would never force himself on anyone.

Yes, he might tease and tempt, but he definitely didn't mind waiting.

He had definitely waited on me.

The things that Delilah said to me that day had my mind in overdrive.

There was just no way that we were talking about the same Tristan.

No, my Tristan didn't have kids.

My Tristan definitely wasn't capable of raping anyone.

She had to be talking about the wrong person.

So, I flew her and Bryson back to Washington so that we could do it all face to face.

Tristan didn't know anything because I didn't want him to try and avoid the confrontation.

I wanted to catch him off guard.

Hell, I wanted some answers and I wanted them now!

With both of them in my car, I drove them to my house and to my surprise, Tristan wasn't there.

I called him in a hurry.

"Hi, where are you?"

"I'll be home in just a second."

Seconds went by, hours went by, and still there was no Tristan.

Where in the hell was he?

Delilah and I basically sat there staring at each other.

The only time either of us spoke was if we were talking to Bryson.

There was nothing really that I wanted or needed to say to her.

She'd said enough already, and I was just ready to get to the bottom of everything.

Finally, he arrived and I waited for him to walk through the door.

"Hey baby," he said before he noticed Delilah.

Once he saw her, Tristan completely froze.

Oh hell no!

He was the same one?

Delilah stared at Tristan.

Tristan stared back at her.

Lord, please tell me that this isn't happening!

This just could not be happening!

Tristan a rapist?

Never!

Tristan is Bryson's father?

Impossible!

"Yes. That's Tristan. The same Tristan that is my son's father and the same Tristan that raped me," Delilah said.

"Raped you? Really Delilah? I didn't rape you. You gave it to me. Just like you always did," Tristan said in a tone of voice that was unfamiliar. His voice was as cold as ice.

Tristan just stared at her, coldly, as if he was asking her what she was doing there. As if he didn't understand her purpose for telling me the truth.

As if he'd wanted to kill her.

Delilah's facial expression had changed as well.

It wasn't the face of a rape victim; in a way it looked as though she was amused or if she'd told the lie on him on purpose as a way of getting under his skin.

Well, he'd admitted to knowing her, and having some kind of sex with her, so I guess she was right.

"Tristan what is she talking about huh? So, it's true? You have a son? You have a child? And by Delilah?"

Tristan didn't say anything for a while.

He stood there. He just looked so damn evil that it was making me more and more uncomfortable.

Finally, after what seemed like forever, he spoke.

"Tori, I have six kids, by six different women."

What the hell did he just say?

Delilah picked up Bryson and sat him on her lap.

It was as if she'd expected things to get ugly. She knew my temper first hand so she must have known that I was liable to swing on him at any given time.

"What do you mean you have six kids Tristan?"

"Just what I said; I have six kids...total. Including him and including the one that my *girlfriend* just had last month. Oh, and I almost forgot about yours. So, I'll have seven kids by seven different women."

What?

Did he just say that his *girlfriend* just had a baby last month?

He couldn't have just said that.

No, my *husband* hadn't just said those words to me.

This had to be a joke.

Someone was playing a joke on me.

I was feeling dizzy, so I sat down.

Tristan just stood by the door and stared at me.

I was at a loss for words, so eventually he spoke up again.

"This was all so easy. I mean how could you not tell that this wasn't what you thought that it was? Well, I guess stretching the whole thing out to over a year, must have been the key to making this all work. I mean surely after the whole house incident I thought that you were going to find me out or at least kick me to the curve but you didn't. I played the part so well, and you believed me. Hell, you even believed her," he said nodding at Delilah.

She shook her head at me as though he was lying but something told me that he wasn't.

What's going on here?

"Not to mention that you believed my other girlfriend too," Tristan said.

What?

His other girlfriend?

So did he have two girlfriends?

What was he talking about?

"Believed who Tristan? The woman at your old house? The one that you said was sold by the bank? That was your *girlfriend*? How? She was married. I saw her husband and I saw her ring."

"You saw what you wanted to see. The husband that you thought you saw was George...her brother-in-law.

She's not married, at least not yet anyway. We were, are, going to get married once you divorce me though. But first I'm leaving with at least half of everything you have. One of those papers that you thought you signed, in regards to the laundromat, wasn't what you thought it was. But you were too tired to read it. Basically, it says that if you divorced me, you agreed to pay me. Sorry, but I didn't do all of this for nothing. But as for her ring, it was the ring that I'd given to you, or didn't you notice? I borrowed it from her. I'm sure she's going to want it back. You must didn't look at it as well as you should have. She played it all off well didn't she? And she was pregnant then, by me of course, but I guess you didn't notice that either." Tristan said.

I wanted to cry but I couldn't.

It was so much to take in all at once and I felt as though my mind and my heart were about to explode.

"The papers that you saw from the bank were fakes. Well, we did find a buyer for the house, but all of the second mortgage crap was a lie. All of the papers that you'd seen, I'd printed up. They were fakes Tori. In fact, every piece of paper that I've ever shown to you was more than likely a fake. My résumé was even a fake. I was never really coming there for a job. I never even really had a job. I haven't worked in years; not a legit job that is. I'd been planning this for a while and when the position come open, I jumped at the opportunity to come in and make my move. Which I did and you fell for it. Why do you think I never answered the calls for the interview? I don't have any of the qualifications and I have a criminal background that's a mile long. Life has been rough for me," Tristan said.

I had to be dreaming.

I looked down at the ring on my finger.

I just had to be dreaming.

This man was *my* husband, and he had become my best friend.

This just could not be happening to me.

I just didn't understand why this was happening to me.

"Why?" I shook my head in disbelief.

"Because you were the only daughter of *his* that was available."

What?

I looked at him confused.

"Your father stole my mother from me. She left me and my father all alone and ran off and made a new family with your Pops without thinking twice about it. I was a young boy. I needed my mother. I was stuck there trying to take care of a dying man that treated me like a dog because of what she'd done to him. It was her job and she'd abandoned us. She completely forgot about me. I've never even heard from her or seen her since the day that she left. The last thing that she said to me was that she loved me...but she loved him more. How do you love someone else's husband more than your own son? My mother wasn't that type of woman. Your father changed her. He seduced her, brainwashed her and she left me behind because of him. So, someone had to pay. And you were the only option. I've known who you were all along. We belonged to the same church...remember? Then again, your mother was so strict on you girls that you wouldn't have been able to look at me back then if I was standing right in your face. You had no idea who I was. And then I found out that you'd done quite well for yourself. You were making the big bucks and you were still single. Someone had to pay for your fathers' actions. And I owed a lot of very bad people a whole lot of money. Thousands of dollars to be exact and they wanted what was due to them, so I had to make a move. They were going to kill me if I didn't pay for the product that was taken when I was busted, so I had to come up with something quick. But you were different than most women. You had so many rules so it took time. It took effort. You weren't as easy to manipulate like I'd hoped you would be. But other than to manipulate you out of money, the only other reason that I thought to marry you was in hopes that your father would show up and bring my mother with him. For years I've been dying to look them both in the face. While I was in prison, I'd learned a few secrets as to how to find people so I knew everything about them and should I say *our* younger brother; but we aren't related. So, I proceeded with my plan. It's your father's fault that she hadn't taken me. He hadn't allowed her to take me with her. She could have at least taken me, her son, even if she didn't love or want to be with my pops. But she didn't. She made her choice. He was her choice. He was the wrong choice. In prison is where I really started following your career and learning a little about accounting, through reading, so that we could be on the same page with you. I had to be ready. You couldn't have possibly thought that I really loved you, did you?"

The sad thing was...I really did.

I felt like all of this was just one, big nightmare that I couldn't wake up from.

There were so many thoughts running wild in my head.

I was humiliated. I was disgusted.

I felt used. But most importantly, I was heartbroken.

How did I miss this?

How could I have not seen any of the signs?

Why hadn't he come with a big, bright, red warning label that said: Danger!

He was a liar, a cheater, a deadbeat, a manipulator, a felon *and* so much more.

He was everything that I hated in a man and more!

I had nothing to do with my father's decisions, nor was I to blame for his mother's actions or hadn't he noticed that?

The choices of my father and his mother affected us too. Hell, it drove my mother insane and it was part of the reason why I looked at men the way that I did.

But as soon as I open my heart and let one in, this is the thanks that I get.

Hell knows no fury like a woman scorned...you got that right!

I didn't look at Tristan or say another word.

I'd heard all that I needed to hear and I didn't need any other explanations.

I stood to my feet and inched forward slowly.

I was heading for the gun in the top of my closet in my shoebox.

Little did he know---he was a dead man.

I didn't look back at him.

I didn't look at Delilah.

I could hear Bryson crying and calling my name but I was on a mission.

I felt as though I was having an out of body experience. It was as if I wasn't walking at all, but more like I was floating.

I was floating towards the bedroom, to get my gun to put a bullet in his head.

The amount of hurt that I felt was so unreal.

My heart was bruised, broken into a thousand small pieces.

I felt as though I could barely breathe.

It was obviously that I could barely walk because it was taking me all of five minutes to make my way down the hallway.

I'd given him everything that I had and he'd used me, played me as if it was okay.

Why would he do this to me?

I had been nothing but good to him.

I finally made it to my closet and I reached in the shoebox for the gun, only to find that it wasn't there.

Where did it go?

Tristan must have found it, which meant that he had to be going through all of my things when I wasn't there.

There was no telling what else he'd found or what else he knew. I was sure he'd been through all of my personal belongings and papers and at this point, who knew what else he was up to.

He'd mentioned getting half of my money but he was just as stupid as he looked.

I hadn't stepped out of our marriage and he didn't have any rights to anything that I had but then again, who knows what he had put in the works.

Who knows what that piece of paper said that he had me sign.

But he wasn't getting a damn thing from me.

He would have to kill me first.

Unable to think straight, I grabbed one of the unused golf clubs that I'd won in a raffle at work one year and headed back to the living room, this time in a hurry.

But I was too late.

He was gone.

And so were Delilah and Bryson.

She'd been playing me too?

She hadn't driven, so she had to have left with Tristan.

What was her point of all the things that she'd said?

What was her point for ratting out Tristan if she was just going to leave with him anyway?

But he raped her right?

Yeah right!

She was up to no good just as much as he was and I'm sure that everything that she'd said had been one big lie.

She had played a part in setting up this whole thing!

I was willing to bet on it and Tristan made it clear that it was something about her that she'd been lying about.

I grabbed my keys and phone and headed out the front door which they'd left standing wide open.

I saw the bear that I'd given to baby Byron lying on the ground in the driveway, as if Tristan had thrown it out the driver's side window.

Speeding, I headed over to *Tristan's house* that his so-called *girlfriend* was still living in but when I got there, the house was vacant and a big blue and white Sold sign was in the yard.

That bastard!

He'd been two steps ahead of me all of this time.

I got out of my car with the club in my hand and headed toward the house anyway.

Without thinking twice about it, I began to smash the windows of the house.

I screamed with every swing that I took.

How could this have happened to me?

What had I done to deserve this?

The neighbors started to come outside and that was my queue to get back into my car and leave.

They chattered as I got into my car and drove away.

It wasn't until I'd been driving into circles for all of five minutes that I began to cry.

I was so hurt.

There were no words to express what I felt.

How could someone be so cruel?

He was my husband.

He was supposed to love me.

He was supposed to care about me. I trusted him and our entire relationship had been a lie.

I stopped at a grocery store parking lot because my vision had become blurred by my tears and I just continued to cry.

I rolled down the window and twisted the ring off of my finger. Without hesitation, I threw it and followed it until it hit hard against the pavement.

I sat staring at it as the tears constantly flowed down my face.

He'd given me another woman's ring?

Who in the hell does that to somebody!

And how stupid was she to let him "borrow" a ring to *fake-marry* someone else?

What the hell is wrong with these people?

Tristan deserved to die for what he'd done to me.

All of them deserved to die.

Reaching for my phone, I dialed his number.

I suddenly had the need to say a bunch of the things that I hadn't been able to say back at the house.

I waited for the phone to ring but instead I heard:

"The number you have reached is no longer in service."

I pulled the phone away from my ear and called Delilah's phone.

And what do you know, I got the same message.

This whole time she had been on his side.

The whole time she had been helping Tristan to prepare to come into my life and ruin me.

She had to have been the one to tell Tristan the type of men that I liked and their style.

She had to have told him my must haves and my pet peeves.

That's why it was so easy for me to fall for him. That's why he'd had me at hello because she'd already told him everything that he'd needed to know.

I knew that she couldn't be trusted but I had no idea that she would have done something like this.

If I ever saw her again, things were going to get ugly. I promise she was going to wear a beat down that she would never forget.

Angry at the world, I threw my phone out of the car window too.

Pieces of it flew in every direction.

Following the battery, my eyes wandered behind me and there I saw the car of the strange woman from the store and the coffee shop that day.

She was still following me?

You have got to be kidding me!

Today was the wrong day for her to stalk me.

And I was going to make sure that she knew it too.

I opened the car door and got out with the golf club in my hand but a few steps in her direction and she started her car and drove off.

Was she Tristan's other girlfriend that he had mentioned?

I screamed at the top of my lungs and the few shoppers that were outside, hurriedly placed their groceries into their cars and got the hell out of there.

This by far was the worst day of my life.

What I felt inside was the worst feeling that I'd ever felt.

I wouldn't wish this amount of pain on my worst enemy.

The hurt just couldn't be put into words.

The betrayal that had just taken place was unreal.

Suddenly, I thought about the baby that was growing inside of me.

There was no way in hell that I was having this baby. I refused to have a child by the Devil.

I wanted to start punching my stomach but my hand wouldn't let me.

I was just going to have to take care of it the regular way.

Dropping the club and placing my hands on my head, I headed back to the car and got in.

There were so many thoughts that were flooding my mind but there was only one feeling flooding my heart.

Hurt.

If this is the heartache and pain that Mama felt as a result of what my father had done to her, I now see why she'd gone crazy.

****

Chapter Eight

Leaving the bank, I was relieved that Tristan hadn't gotten ahold of anything that he wasn't supposed to.

I switched all of my bank accounts and I'd even tried to stop the payment on the $60,000 check that I'd written Tristan for the laundromats, but it had already been cashed.

He'd made it clear that he'd lied about everything, so there weren't going to be any laundromats, I'm sure. He must have needed the money, and more to pay back whoever it was that he owed money to.

But I wasn't going to sweat it.

In my book, it was chump change compared to what I still had, so I simply counted it as a loss.

And as far as the marriage goes, I'd found the certificate on top of the refrigerator.

I'd forgotten to turn it in.

Tristan was supposed to do it but said something about a run that day and instead asked me to drop it off. Only I'd started eating and completely forgot about it.

So guess what that means....that's right, we were *never* legally married.

I was never legally married to that bastard.

Though my mother had performed the ceremony, it wasn't legal without the turning in of the certificate and that certificate was long gone.

I'd torn it to pieces.

I didn't have to go through a divorce.

I didn't have to go through an annulment.

I didn't have to do anything.

Tristan didn't have any rights, to anything that belonged to me. I wasn't his wife and all was completely well in that category.

Screw whatever piece of paper he thought that he had.

That piece of good news had even managed to make me smile though it had only been days since everything had happened and my heart was still completely shattered.

I'd spent all of three days, locked inside of the house, sitting in the dark.

I couldn't do anything.

I couldn't eat.

I couldn't sleep.

I hadn't even bothered to bathe for those three days.

I just sat there, all day and all night, thinking about what had happened to me.

The one thing that I had managed to do was mess up all of Tristan's things.

I'd bleached, ripped, cut, or burned everything of Tristan's that was in my house and placed it in trash bags on the side of the street.

I'd cried until I couldn't cry anymore.

I was lower than I'd ever been in my entire life.

I even went without getting a new phone for those three days. I didn't want to talk to anyone because no one could help me.

No one could heal me.

And then on day number four, something told me to stop crying, to stop feeling sorry for myself and to get up and do what needed to be done.

So, that's what I had done.

The only thing left to handle now was the baby...the abortion.

It was against every belief that I had but I didn't have a choice.

There was no way that I was going to be able to have this baby.

I wouldn't be able to look at it without thinking of Tristan and what he'd done to me.

I wouldn't want it to have to pay for its father's mistakes like I'd just had to pay for mine.

After finally getting a new phone, I decided that I needed to talk to someone about the abortion subject so I asked my mother and my sister Cheyanne to meet me for lunch.

"Where have you been? And why do you look so bad? Are you still sick? I've been calling you for days," my sister Cheyanne asked all at once.

My mother just sat looking at me.

With all eyes on me, right in front of the waiter, I started to cry uncontrollably.

I hadn't cried in a whole day but it all just hit me all over again as I tried to explain the situation to them through my tears.

My sister tried to comfort me, but my mother just sat there looking at me as if I was a stranger.

"It's not so easy to see the *signs* when you're the one in the midst of the storm...is it?" Mama asked.

What?

I looked at her confused.

"You used to ask me all the time, how couldn't I tell and how didn't I know what your father was doing behind my back. You would often say that you didn't know how I missed it but it's not so easy to see the truth when you're the one in the dummy slot is it Tori?"

I almost became upset by her comments, but she was right.

Though I didn't want to hear it, she was right.

I had been blinded by love and because he was doing and saying all of the right things, I'd forgotten to see the signs that were clearly there.

I was blinded by love for the first and the last time.

The other times I'd ended up in situations didn't count since I hadn't really loved them in the first place.

"You've lived your whole life by rules and standards and the moment you tried to adjust yourself, you hurt yourself. You thought you were missing out and instead of waiting you thought that if you changed who you were and dropped some of your requirements, that you would have what everyone else has. But the truth is you had so much more. You had your pride, your dignity and your self-respect. Tori, you were fine just the way that you were," my mother said.

I smiled at her and I knew that yet again she was right.

"People talked about me and called me crazy for years. It was the way that I chose to deal with the hurt. I let it beat me but you won't. You won't be me. You will get through this. You will get over this. Get your morals and your standards back and you will be just fine. You have to do the one thing that you've always told everyone else to do. You have to always, no matter what, pay attention to those signs."

To be honest, I didn't want to pay attention to anything.

After this, I don't think that I ever want to even think about being in love again.

Before, I had done just fine without it.

I wasn't the happiest but I was happy.

I was going back to my old self.

And my old self says:

Love was for suckers!

We chatted a little while longer and then my mother spoke again.

"Something you said seemed off. You didn't know the whole time that he was the Deacon's and your daddy's mistress's son?"

I looked at mama confused.

Hell no I didn't know!

First of all, that would have been too close to home for me. I mean that would have made him almost like, I mean technically, my step brother.

Of course I didn't know!

"Of course I didn't know that. Wait a minute, are you saying that you did?"

"Yes, he's older but he's still the young man from the church back then."

I looked at Mama in disbelief.

"Why didn't you say something Mama?"

"He told me that you knew," she said and took a sip of her tea.

He was going straight to hell!

***

As I laid still, on the abortion table, I thought about my mother.

I still couldn't believe that she'd known who Tristan was and hadn't mentioned it.

Even if he'd told her that we'd had the conversation, she still could have mentioned to me.

Though I hadn't asked, I could help but wonder how I'd missed the topic.

Where had I been when the conversation had taken place?

Then it hit me.

It had to be the first time that I took Tristan to meet her and I'd had to leave to make a quick run to the office.

Yes, that must have been when the conversation happened.

Still, mama said that she had no idea that I hadn't remembered him and that she'd known who he was the very first time that she'd saw him.

She'd said that he told her that we'd talked through it and decided to pursue the relationship anyway.

Not to mention that mama said that she hadn't seen a problem with it because his mother was dead.

So the whole step-brother mess was out the window.

I asked her how she knew that Tristan's mama had died and she said it was because she'd reached out to my father.

She'd said in order to be completely free, she'd needed to talk to him so she'd asked for his information from Tristan a few days before the surprise wedding.

After calling numerous of times, she was finally able to reach my father two days after the ceremony and he'd told her that Tristan's mother had been dead for over two years.

She'd assumed that Tristan had known this, but I was sure that he didn't.

And then again, maybe he did which would have been an even bigger reason to come at me and take me through what he'd done to me.

The truth is, no one knew all of the details and since I was sure that Tristan and Delilah were long gone, I probably never would.

All I knew was what he'd told me and said to me that day. I would never forget any of his words and I would never forget what he'd done to me.

But mama had been right.

I still had time.

I still had my whole life to live and I was going to beat this.

I was going to win.

So, the first step to getting on with my life was getting rid of this baby.

I'd thought about it long and hard and this was the best thing for me to do.

With my sister Cheyanne by my side, the doctor that my sister Lauren suggested, entered and we were ready to get the process done and over with.

"I can't find a heartbeat. Let's have a look shall we," the doctor said as the nurse got me ready for an ultrasound.

He rubbed the cool jelly on my stomach and soon the tiny little fetus showed up on the screen.

The doctor was silent for just a second and then he spoke.

"Well, the fetus is already dead. I'm surprised you haven't started the miscarriage process. We can go ahead and clean it out for you or you can let your body and the miscarriage naturally run its course."

It seemed as though no sooner than he'd said the words, I got a sharp pain in the side of my belly.

I got up from the table slowly, thanking God that he'd already worked it out before I'd had to do something that I probably would've regretted later.

He was always on time.

My office looked like a flower shop.

It seemed as though folks were still bringing in flowers every day.

The long stem red roses were still piling up on my desk.

And the first thing I did was throw each and every one of them in the trash.

As far as I was concerned they were from Tristan and I didn't need anything reminding me of him.

"Glad to have you back. Now can we get some work done? You know that you're my best gal. Things aren't the same when you're not running the show," my boss Hunter said.

I smiled at him and nodded.

I was back to my regular old life and my regular routine.

And to be honest, it wasn't all that bad.

Actually, it wasn't bad at all.

Things were going to be normal again; my kind of normal, although it wasn't exactly normal to everyone else.

And I was going to be okay.

The work day went by swiftly and so did the rest of the week. Before I knew it, it was Friday and the end of the work week.

I'd kept myself busy and I'd only been home pretty much to shower and to sleep.

My house just didn't feel the same and I was currently looking for something new.

It was around seven in the evening and I prepared myself to go.

Though it wasn't exactly too late, I still waited for the janitor to finish doing what he was doing before going out the door.

When he noticed me, I headed out the door and he made his way to the window.

I got into the car and he turned away.

Just as I started to drive off, there was a knock on my window.

It was the woman that had been following me.

The first thought that went through my mind was to get out and give her a piece of my mind, and maybe even whoop her ass for following folks like she didn't have any home training, but then I thought what if this was some kind of set up or something.

What if she was really connected to Tristan?

I was sure that by now he had tried to pursue whatever legal action that he was up to from the singed paper but had found out that I wasn't even his wife, so there was no telling what he could have been trying to plan to get even with me.

He knew that I knew all of them but since I'd never mention the woman following me, maybe he was trying to send in a new face.

No one could be trusted these days and it had already been established that she was a stalker, which clearly said that the bitch had issues, so I wasn't going to take any chances.

It wasn't that I was scared or anything but I wasn't going to be stupid.

Not again.

I didn't even attempt to ask her what she wanted, I simply drove off.

I glanced behind me to see if she was following me. I didn't see her, but I was positive that she knew where I lived, so I headed to Cheyanne's instead.

I stayed at her house with her, while her husband went to my place to retrieve some of my things.

"So, you're going to move?"

"Yes, I'm not going back there. With everything thing that happened with Tristan, and with this strange woman following me, I just don't know what's going to happen next. I'm pretty sure it has something to do with him but I don't care what it is. I just want to be left alone. I just want to forget about it all and move on."

"Well, you can stay here as long as you need to. It'll be nice having you around," Cheyanne said.

I grinned as she headed to pour us both a drink.

Her phone started to vibrate and her husband's picture showed up.

I answered it just in case he needed help finding something for me.

"Hello?"

"Cheyanne? Why have you been ignoring me? I still want the money that you owe me."

I knew that voice.

It was Tristan.

I moved the phone away from my ear and looked at the number.

It was a number that I didn't recognize but it was definitely Tristan.

She must've saved his new number under her husband's contact information as a way of trying to keep it hidden.

"Cheyanne?"

I didn't respond.

I simply hung up.

What did he mean when he said that he wanted his money?

Cheyanne returned with a smile on her face and two wine glasses filled to the rim.

"Okay, now, if this doesn't make you feel better, I don't know what will," she teased.

Her phone started to vibrate again.

She looked at it and saw that it was her husband's face on the screen, but we both knew that it wasn't her husband.

She waved it off as if to say that he didn't want anything but she wasn't getting off that easy.

"It's probably Tristan again. You should answer it."

She looked at me as though I was a talking about a person that had come back from the dead.

She sat down her drink and scooted closer to me but I stood up.

"Pay him? He said you still had to pay him what you owed him. Pay him for what Cheyanne?"

She looked at me as though she was going to cry as she started shaking her head.

"Pay him for what?"

"I swear, I didn't know about all of the other stuff," she said.

"Pay him for what?" I asked her again.

"I'm sorry. I'm so sorry."

I didn't say a word.

I waited for her to speak.

"I met him a while before you did. He approached me, and with what he told you, I'm assuming it was to see if I was married and I was. I had no idea who he was or what his *real* intentions were."

I still didn't say a word.

"So, although I was married, we---,"she paused.

Please don't tell me that they had sex!

Lord you wouldn't put that much on me.

"It was only once."

Unbelievable!

What was the world coming to?

I'd always known that my sister had a few tendencies. She was more than flirtatious and I wouldn't doubt if at least one of her kids weren't her husbands, but to have screwed a man, that I ended up dating, screwing, half-way marrying and getting pregnant by, and not say anything, was a bit much.

The tears were burning my eyes but I dared not let them fall.

"I was so angry with you. It all happened so fast. Do you remember that day a long time ago that you asked me to go over to your house and bring you a different pair of shoes to your job because the heel broke on the ones that you were wearing? Well, that day I went over and I was just messing around in your closet. You have a thousand pairs of shoes, so at first I was just trying on a few."

She stopped for only a second because she thought she heard her husband's car outside. When she didn't hear a car door close, she continued.

"I was just messing like I always do when you are there. But I came across a bag full of pictures. I looked at a few and then I noticed that there was a journal. I wasn't going to read it but I figured that I probably knew everything in it anyway. Except I didn't. I found the page where you talked about our sister, Lauren, screwing around with my ex-fiancé Rodney, right under my nose. Yes I know you told me to drop him, but you hadn't told me the whole truth and I was angry. I was so angry at you and at her. I was just angry."

I shook my head at the amount of stupidity that surrounded me.

I saved her from an awful marriage.

Did it really matter who he had been sticking his piece of meat in?

The important part was that I'd warned her and I'd saved her from making a huge mistake.

Whatever happened to just being thankful?

"Anyway, that same day, I ran into Tristan, again, at the store on my way home. I wanted you to be wrong. You were always right when it came to men. You thought you knew every little thing and I just wanted you to be wrong for once. So, I made him a little proposition. I told him about you and that I wanted him to make you fall in love with him and then dump you. I already knew he was the bad boy type so I'd warned him to clean up. We talked regularly for a week or so and I gave him as much information on you as I could. He was supposed to accidently run into at a store, but the whole interviewing for a job thing, I had nothing to do with that. I swear I didn't. It was supposed to be short lived; a few months at the most just to prove you wrong. I wasn't even sure if you would fall for him. He'd said that he would do it but of course for a price. I'd also been having an affair with my married gynecologist for the last few years, so I have a decent stash of *mad* money. He pays me for my *services* just like my insurance pays him for his. Anyway, five thousand dollars is what we'd agreed on. I'd only given him half up front. I thought he was just going to fool you and be done with the whole thing but things just went way too far. He'd convinced me that he'd really fallen for you and I believed him. So at the time, he told me I didn't owe him the rest of the money and I never paid him. The deal was off the table because he told me that he'd really fallen in love with you. I felt bad but I thought that you guys really hit it off and you were so happy, so we never spoke of it again. And then when everything blew up and his truths came out, he called me wanting the other half of money. He'd said he needed it to go with the rest of his money to start his new life. And then he'd said that if I didn't double it, he was going to tell my husband about us."

Honestly, I hoped he did.

I hoped he exposed her for the lying, conniving, slut that she was.

Of all people, never would I have guessed that she would have done something like this to me.

After all that I'd done for her.

We were sisters.

How could she intentionally try to hurt me?

Why would she want to do that to me?

People do the craziest things to the people that love them the most but they will give their whole heart and all of their loyalty, to someone who barely gives a damn about them.

I'll never understand it.

I didn't comment to anything that she'd said.

I grabbed my purse and headed towards the door.

"I'm so sorry Tori. I didn't know that things were going to happen the way that they did. I didn't mean it. I didn't know that he already knew who we were and that he was really out to hurt any one of us before any offer was on the table. It was stupid and I'm so sorry. I love you so much," Cheyanne cried but I walked out of the front door and didn't look back.

Her husband pulled into the driveway.

Quietly, I took the things from his car and transferred them to mine.

Without saying a word, once I was done, I drove away.

****

Chapter Nine

"Let me guess, you're staying late again?" Hunter asked.

I simply nodded.

He didn't respond, just shook his head and headed in the direction of his mistress, who was waiting for him a few feet away.

Men make me sick.

I hadn't spoken to my sister in over a week since finding out that she had intentionally tried to hurt me by paying and sending Tristan my way.

Little did she know, he was already hot on our trail and I had long since been his *target.*

He'd basically just used her offer as an opportunity to make some extra cash.

She'd made a deal with the Devil.

And the thought that she'd had sex with him bothered me even more than finding out what she'd done.

It was nasty as hell, and since being told, I always felt so dirty.

My showers were twice as long and I could barely stand to look at myself in the mirror.

I guess the best way to describe it is that I felt like a hand-me-down, or second best.

The whole situation definitely had me feeling like I was a stranger in my own body.

Of course I hadn't heard anything from Tristan or Delilah and I could only hope that I would never see them another day in my entire life.

I would probably catch a charge if I did.

It would be a dream come true to run both of them over with my car.

Prison would probably feel more like home to me these days anyway; especially since my house no longer felt like a home.

Speaking of, I still hadn't been staying at my place.

I was staying at a hotel, just walking distance from my job.

I was for sure that I was going to sell it, but first I had to find another place...in Charlotte, North Carolina.

Our firm had a *sister-company* there and I was talking with a few people in that office about a transfer.

Of course it was ideal for the Senior Vice President to be located here at the main company, but they would be okay without me.

So, it wasn't really a matter of if it was possible...it was.

It was just a matter of when.

When would I be ready to make that move?

The truth was, I was ready now.

There was nothing left for me here and I only imagined that in the next month or two, I would be hitting the road and never looking back.

"You don't like roses do you?"

The night janitor asked as he emptied my trashcan.

I was still getting the roses at least once a week.

I'd called the shop on the bottom of the vase and they'd told me that they had been preordered a while ago to be delivered randomly for the next few months.

Of course they wouldn't give me any information on the buyer, but it had Tristan's name written all over it. He was always doing things like this to flatter me, but unfortunately it was all one big scheme.

"I do, but my favorite is lilies," I said to him.

He shook his head and continued to do his job.

He seemed nice.

He also seemed shy.

He never really gave eye contact even when we briefly spoke.

I could tell that he had a kind spirit about him. He spoke when spoken to and towards me he had always been friendly.

Just then, I wondered if he would be okay with being just a little friendlier than usual by answering a few of my questions about men.

I would love to hear a male's point of view about a few things.

It was just us left in the office as always, so hopefully he wouldn't mind chatting with me a little.

"Can I ask you something?"

"Sure."

"What's the secret? What is it that men truly want from a woman?"

He placed the trashcan back down by my desk and then he answered.

"Men want the same thing women want. Love, loyalty, honest and respect. Our approaches to obtaining it are just different," he said.

I thought about his comment.

"But why are men so cruel? They can hurt a woman and break her heart and not think twice about it?"

"Some women are the same way."

"Yeah, but mostly its men. They can have a woman that gives them all of the things that you said and still play her and try to run game on her."

"Well, if he's trying to play her and run game on her, than clearly she just isn't the one. If she was the one he wouldn't do a thing to lose her. It just depends on the man and what he truly wants," he said heading towards the door.

"But then why don't they just say that? Why don't they just say what they want?"

"Some do. Some don't. Some show all of the right signs, and give all of the right vibes, and some women just miss them. They see what they want to see."

No he didn't try to throw the signs thing in my face!

I didn't need any advice on recognizing the signs.

I had that covered.

Tristan had been the first love and the last love to catch me slipping and off of my toes.

"Maybe."

"Yeah, maybe."

The janitor walked out of my office, closing the door behind him.

Though I hadn't gotten too much out of him, he seemed like he might have a little knowledge that might be beneficial to me in the future.

Maybe with him more often wouldn't be such a bad idea, especially if I wanted something worth having in the future.

The insight would be good.

At the moment, I couldn't even imagine dating, touching, or even looking at a man in that way, but one day I'm sure that I might be ready again.

I found it funny that he'd mentioned signs.

Did he know who he was talking to?

I was the queen at recognizing them.

It was only when the man had a head's up or help like Tristan had been given, that I'd missed them.

For instance, the nonchalant communication, and even the failure to look me in my face for longer than a second, told me that he, the janitor, was probably one of the few men that were happy in whatever relationship that he was in.

He left little, to no room, for messing up.

The only other men that I'd seen that in were one of my brother's and both of my sister's husbands'.

Nevertheless, talking to him may help me in the future so I planned to small talk with him as much as possible.

Who knows, maybe he could teach me something.

I stayed as late as my mind would allow me to that night and finally I headed to the front door.

The janitor noticed me heading in that direction and made his way to the window.

I figured that if I was going to try to get him to tell me all of the secrets about men, I at least needed to know his name.

Just before heading out the door I turned back to him.

"By the way, what's your name?"

"Everyone calls me Freeman," he said.

"Well, though you know me as Miss Young, Freeman, I'm Tori. Nice to officially meet you," I smiled and headed out the door.

I didn't bother to look back because I knew that he would watch me until I was safe inside my car.

To think about it, that was more than nice of him.

***

"I know you have been through a lot but at least talk to her. Work it out. She's still your sister and family is all that matters at the end of the day," my mother preached.

I heard her.

But I didn't care what she was saying.

I knew eventually that I would have to speak to my sister again, but for right now, I just needed space.

"Mama, I have to tell you something."

My mother looked at me attentively.

"I'm moving away."

Her face expression was a mixture of frustration and confusion or maybe it was more along the lines of disapproving.

"Tori, why are you running away? Running won't make you forget what happened to you and running won't heal your broken heart."

Mama was right, but it was a start.

It seemed like everything and everywhere reminded me of the humiliation and betrayal that Tristan, Delilah and Cheyanne had caused me.

I just needed to get away so that I could fully recover and get back to being me.

I didn't bother continuing the conversation with my mother because my mind was already made up.

I was leaving as soon as I could and nothing was going to change my mind about it.

After leaving my mother's apartment, I finally decided that it was time to go back home.

I'd gotten me another gun while I was staying at the hotel and if anyone so much as acted like they were going to bother me, they were going to be pumped full of lead before they could even make the first move.

Walking in the front door, I felt as though I'd just walked into a funeral home.

The house felt dead.

It didn't feel lively at all.

I instantly became sad all over again.

Yes, I was going to have to get away from here. There was just no other way around it.

I forced myself to give the house a good cleaning and then I made myself dinner from the few items that were still in the refrigerator.

Even cooking didn't seem to change my mood.

After dinner, I poured myself a glass of wine and ran myself a bath.

I'll admit, in my own home, I was a little bit nervous to just sit and relax in my own tub but I pushed my feelings of worry aside and forced myself enjoy the moment.

I was so tired of thinking about the same things over and over again so I forced myself to think about the future.

I couldn't help but wonder what was in store for me.

I was now thirty and my life plan wasn't turning out the way that I'd thought that it would be.

But I still had a chance.

There was no point in crying over spilled milk. There was no point to still be in a state of depression.

The old *me* was amazing.

The old me was strong and could bounce back from anything.

I loved who I was and though most times, I only had myself to depend on, myself was enough.

I didn't need anybody to validate me.

I could validate my damn self.

Tori, you are going to be just fine. You are strong, and you are beautiful. You are independent, reliable and you have more than enough to offer, anyone, at any time...anywhere.

I reminded myself of these things over and over again.

It seemed like the more I thought them, the more I built up my self-esteem.

The more I thought them, the more confidence and power over my life and situation I got back.

The more I thought them, the more that I knew that I was a winner. I could be bent, but I couldn't be broken.

I had always been a winner and now wasn't the time to start losing.

I was Tori Marie Young, and I was back!

For the first time in what seemed like such a long time, I smiled.

I was back.

My life was going to get back on track and I was back to the basics.

And speaking of, since I was back to the basics, I had a sudden idea or maybe it was a sudden urge.

I got out of the tub and headed to my dresser.

Well, hello Bo...I don't know what I was thinking to have ever left you, I thought as I turned the switch to on and laid on my back to enjoy my two minutes of pleasure.

Damn, I'd miss my Bo.

***

"I hadn't seen you smile in a long time," the janitor, I meant, Freeman said.

"Oh, you'd noticed?"

"Everyone had. It was quite the buzz all over the office as to what might be going on with you," he said.

We were the only two left in the building, as always, and we'd starting chatting a lot more than usual.

He was actually very smart for a janitor.

Not rocket science smart, but smarter than I thought that he would be.

"Well, I'm fine. All is fine."

He continued getting my office together and then he turned around to face me

"Are you happily single?" he asked.

"What made you think I was single?"

"Oh sorry, I just assumed."

"You shouldn't assume. But you're right. I am single. And had you asked me that a while ago, I would have said no. All I thought about was finding love and wondered if the perfect love actually existed. I still don't know the answer to that but to answer your question, yes. Yes, I'm okay with being single. Love will happen when it's supposed to. It's when you rush it that you end up in a bad situation," I answered him honestly.

"And what does a woman like you who has everything actually want when it comes to love or a man?" He asked.

I was surprised.

Usually I was the one asking him a thousand questions.

I thought about his question.

I was surprised at how much my thoughts and the way that I saw things had changed in the last month or so.

I could have said that the perfect man had to have at least a salaried job, a 401k, no kids and a list of other things, but here lately, my list had been revised.

"All I would want is love; real, true, and indescribable love...to hell with everything else."

He smiled.

"Good answer."

Leaving work that night, I couldn't help but thank God for the way that I was feeling.

I couldn't help but tell him how thankful that I was to be feeling like myself again, but a better, more mature version.

I knew now that all that I had gone through had only been a test and despite all of the odds, I passed it.

There was just one last thing that I had to do.

"Hi."

"Hi."

"Tori, I've missed you so much. I'm so sorry. I---,"

"Cheyanne?"

My sister took a deep breath.

"Yes?" she sobbed.

"I love you."

And with that I hung up the phone.

I wasn't sure of what else to say or if our relationship would ever be the same, but I knew that I had to forgive her and I knew that I had to let go of the hurt that she'd caused me in order to truly be free.

She was my sister and no matter what, she always would be. And no matter what I still loved her.

That was it.

I felt the last ounce of weight that had been resting on my shoulders, float away.

Everything was going to be just fine.

I was sure of it.

The next morning, I headed out the door early.

I was so excited that I couldn't sleep the night before.

Today was the day that I was going to announce to everyone at work that I would be transferring to Charlotte.

I hadn't found a buyer for the house, since I'd talked my mother into giving up her apartment and just living in my house for free.

I would still pay the utilities and things of that nature, and that way, if for some reason I ever wanted to come back, I wouldn't have to go through the buying a house struggle all over again.

But for some reason, I knew in the bottom of my heart that I was never coming back.

At least not to live.

It was just time for me to go.

Maybe in Charlotte, there was a husband somewhere there waiting for me.

Even though I was on a *love strike*, still, I wasn't giving up on love.

I wasn't giving up on a happy life and a future filled with a husband and kids.

But this time, I wasn't giving up any of myself either.

I wanted it all.

I hadn't found a house to buy yet in North Carolina, but I'd managed to find one to rent until I could get there and learn the area.

Life was only about to get better.

I stopped at the coffee shop across the street from work, one last time for my expresso.

I smiled as the taste harassed my tonsils as I walked out the glass doors.

"Excuse me."

I turned around.

For some reason, my heart felt as though it had dropped out of my chest into the pit of my stomach.

It was the woman that had been stalking me for what seemed like almost a year now.

I clutch my purse.

I was *packing* and one wrong move and she was going to have a very bad day.

This was the first time that I actually looked her in the face.

She was very pretty.

She wore a lot of make-up but you could tell that it was the expensive kind and the long weave in her hair was just as pricey.

To be honest, she looked like a model.

Her frame was tall and slim like one too.

"Who are you and why have you been following me all of this time? Do I know you or something?"

"No."

"Then what is it?"

She was quiet for a second.

I could tell that she was no threat but I still wanted to know what the hell it was that she wanted.

"Actually, standing here, something just hit me. All of this time, I'd gone through the trouble of figuring out who you were. I was upset that he'd chosen you, when really I had no reason to be angry with you in the first place. I should have been angry with him."

Lord, I knew that she had something to do with Tristan.

My guess was that she was one of his baby's mamas or that other girlfriend that he'd mentioned.

"I'm sorry to have ever had bothered you. It finally dawned on me that I deserve better. He loves you, not me and I finally need to just accept it. I wish you and Brass all of the best of luck," she said and turned and speedily walked away.

What?

Who the hell is *Brass*?

I was going to call after her, but I let her go.

I didn't know anyone named Brass.

I couldn't help but chuckle.

She'd been following and stalking the wrong person all of this time...how crazy is that?

When all she'd had to do in the first place was just ask.

And then I thought about it.

Maybe Brass was Tristan's real name or something.

There was no telling what all he'd lied about but I shrugged my shoulders.

I didn't have to worry about her anymore from what she'd said and the fact that I was moving anyway confirmed it, just in case she changed her mind.

Settling into my office, I sent Hunter an email.

I'd wanted to be the one to tell him and I wanted to tell him first before telling the rest of the office.

With a knock on the door, I looked up with a smile expecting to see Hunter, but instead I saw the janitor...Freeman.

I looked at him confused.

Freeman was dressed in an all-black Armani suit.

I knew Armani when I saw it.

What I didn't understand is how a janitor could afford it and why he was dressed that way.

I smiled as I noticed that he was holding a vase full of lilies.

"Hi."

"Hi."

"These are for you," he said walking towards me and reached me the vase.

Immediately I recognized that it was the same vase that once held the roses but I checked the label on the bottom to be sure.

Yep.

"It was you who were sending the roses?" I asked.

He nodded.

"Why?"

"Well, over a year ago, I walked into this building and I saw the woman that I was destined to marry. The way you walked. The way you dressed. The way you tilted your head back when you laughed or the way you squinted your eyes when you smiled. I'd come in to meet with Hunter for the first time but I just knew that I had to have you."

I was lost.

I was so confused.

Surely if I'd saw him dressed like that I would have noticed.

"I don't understand."

"Well, I don't know if you've noticed but I'm a little on the shy side. I'm terrible when it comes to speaking and talking to women. But here lately you have helped me with that. I'd asked Hunter to introduce me, but he'd said that you hadn't budged at the invitation to get set up by him so, I went to plan B."

Plan B?

What exactly was Plan A?

I was so confused.

"You see, I'm technically not a janitor. I actually own the company. The janitors, the whole cleaning staff of this company are contracted hires of my company. My father left it to me. Well over a year ago he passed away and I'd come to meet with Hunter for the first time. I have employees at over 50 facilities, just in Washington alone, and I'd just wanted to take the time to come and introduce myself as the new face of the company. But when I saw you, you were all that I could think about. I wanted to be near you and as Hunter put it, that wouldn't be an easy thing to do, so I took on the role as playing a janitor. I'd come in the day time just to see you and watch you from a distance. And when Hunter told me that you would mostly stay all night, I'd made him agree to let me know so that I could come in just to be here with you. I would only stay until I watched you leave. No matter how late you stayed, I would stay right here until you left. After you were gone, the real janitor would come and resume his position."

I couldn't believe my ears.

Who would have thought?

What I was hearing was like a mixture of flattery and obsession, but for some reason, it made me feel good in the inside.

"I hope I'm not freaking you out. It was just something about you. I wanted to talk to you so many times and little by little you begin to notice me. And then here lately, we somewhat have become the best of friends. To be honest, the whole pretend to be a janitor may have been a bit extreme, but aside of being nervous to approach you I wanted you to see me for me. I wanted to see if you would see a janitor. And you did. You actually saw me. All of my life, people have only seen me as a dollar sign. My father started this company thirty years ago, and I was left with millions, but I didn't want you to see that part of me. I just wanted you to just see me. When you started speaking to me, more so than anyone else ever took the time to, I knew that you were special. You always told me thank you, even if you were extremely busy. And then finally, you started to hold conversations with me and ask me questions. I finally got to know a little of you and you were able to see a part of me. But what made me realize that it was time was your comment the other night. The one when you said the only thing that you wanted was love. You didn't say money. You didn't say comfort or stability. All you said was love. I knew that it was time to make my move. I knew that it was time for me to love you."

My mouth dropped open.

At that moment, I was reminded of a saying that mama would say to us when we were younger.

She would say that when you were down to nothing, God was always up to something.

And right here, right now, that was the only thing that I could think about.

I didn't know what to say or what to do.

"So you're single?" I finally managed to ask him.

I'd always assumed that he was taken by the way that he'd acted so I'd never even asked him about his personal life.

"Very. I was in a relationship, but I broke it off a long time ago. I'm a praying man. A man of faith, and something just told me that she wasn't the one...you were," he said.

So this is what the old folks meant when they said that you didn't have to go looking, your Boaz would find you?

What was I supposed to do with all of this?

What was I supposed to say?

"Tori, you needed to see me? Oh Hi Brass! So you finally talked to her huh?" Hunter said entering my office.

Brass?

Freeman...was Brass?

So the woman that had been stalking me had been stalking me because of him?

Huh?

"I thought your name was Freeman."

"It is...but everybody calls me Brass. It's a nickname given to me by my father," he said.

So, she was right.

She'd said that he'd left her for me and that he loved me.

He loved me?

How?

Why?

"See Tori, I'd tried to introduce you to him. He's a damn good guy. Any man that walks around picking up trash, just to get your attention, deserves a shot, or at least a date," Hunter joked.

I was still trying to take it all in.

I only knew him from the talks that we'd started having but just from those alone, I knew that he was a good catch.

He'd pretended to be a janitor, all for me, and I couldn't see it.

Had it not been for the heartbreak of Tristan, I'd probably never started having the deep conversations with him. I probably would have never gotten to know how amazing he was.

I guess everything that happens, does happen for a reason huh?

But who does something like this for a woman that they didn't even know?

And all because of his faith?

I looked at the lilies.

He'd been sending me flowers for months...how special and committed was that?

Every sign and everything about him pointed towards happiness.

I know, I'd been fooled before, but something told me that this, and that he, was different.

I could feel it in my gut and my gut was telling me to take a chance.

"Tori, what was it that you wanted to tell me?" Hunter asked again.

That's right.

I was supposed to be moving to Charlotte.

I couldn't leave now.

I couldn't move after all of this could I?

I couldn't move after what he'd just said.

Hell no I couldn't!

My Boaz was here and so this is where I had to be.

"Oh, never mind," I said to him.

The truth was that I could always move in the future if I needed to but looking at the man in front of me, the chances of that happening were slim to none.

"So Tori, I've waited for a long time to ask you this. Can I take you to get some breakfast?" Freeman-Brass, ask.

I looked at Hunter.

He smiled and winked his eye, giving me the go ahead.

I smiled back and took a deep breath.

Here we go.

This was it.

I was taking another chance on love and this time, I knew that love was going to be kind to me.

He grabbed my hand and walked me out of the building.

He pressed the alarm on the black Benz and walked around to the passenger side to open my door.

I took another deep breath, smiled and got in.

I fastened my seat belt, and as he got in on the other side, I glanced across the street at the coffee shop.

And...

There they were.

It was Tristan, Delilah, Bryson and the woman from the house that day.

Tristan and Delilah were hand and hand, while the woman from the house held hands with Bryson.

They were all laughing and smiling.

I couldn't figure out if they had some kind of freaky relationship, or if they'd lied about who the woman actually was, but Tristan held the door for them all to enter and then kissed Delilah as she entered last.

They looked happy.

They really, really did.

I'd always thought that I would feel hatred and anger if I ever saw them again, but I didn't.

I felt nothing.

It was a miracle.

I felt absolutely nothing.

I was free!

"Are you okay?" Freeman-Brass asked.

I took on last look and turned away from the coffee shop to face him.

I smiled and grabbed his hand.

"I've never been better," I said and he smiled as we drove away.

****

The End

For more books by this author search B.M. Hardin on Amazon.com

Author's Next Release: "The Hush Hotel" coming in June!

Subscribe to book releases at:

www.savvilypblished.com/contact

CPSIA information can be obtained at www.ICGtesting.com
Printed in the USA
LVOW11s1700011015

456528LV00002B/514/P